Karl Hahn's MP-5 slipped from his fingers

The weapon dangled uselessly by its nylon lanyard as Hahn was knocked to the ground by the Australian. The gunman immediately worked the barrel of his rifle under Hahn's chin.

The Phoenix Force pro braced his palms against the weapon to prevent it from choking him, but leverage and gravity were on the killer's side.

As the man leaned forward, exerting more pressure on the rifle, Hahn's arms bent at the elbows. The rifle slowly inched nearer its goal. Hahn's eyes bulged, and his temples pulsed as he struggled to prevent the inevitable.

Then Hahn felt the edge of the rifle settle on his throat!

Mack Bolan's
PHOENIX FORCE

PHOENIX FORCE

Down Under Thunder

Gar Wilson

A GOLD EAGLE BOOK FROM

WORLDWIDE

TORONTO · NEW YORK · LONDON · PARIS
AMSTERDAM · STOCKHOLM · HAMBURG
ATHENS · MILAN · TOKYO · SYDNEY

First edition September 1986

ISBN 0-373-61325-3

Special thanks and acknowledgment to
Paul Glen Neuman for his contributions to this work.

Printed in Canada

1

The dingoes were hungry.

A howl broke through the stillness of the night as the bleeding man ran faster. Around him the dunes of the outback stretched endlessly in all directions. He stumbled and fell, his knees sinking into the sand. Another howl sounded from behind. The eerie call was much closer this time, but the wounded man refused to glance over his shoulder. Wearily he dragged himself to his feet and clawed his way to the top of the dune.

It was August. It was winter. Stars decorated the evening sky in clusters of unfamiliar constellations. Gerry Stabler blinked and shook his head as tears washed some of the stinging grit from his eyes. His teeth and tongue were coated with sand. He pressed his fingers to the pain at his side and tried to ignore the sticky warmth that he felt there. He scrambled over the top of the dune and kept on going.

Applegate and Curtis were dead. Both of Stabler's colleagues had been shot in the head with the same weapon that had blasted the leaking hole in his side. Stabler grunted as his heart pounded in his chest. His partners had accepted their fate too easily; it was almost as if they had welcomed it.

Stabler respected himself and his mission too much to surrender without a fight. When the killer's gun was trained on him, Stabler had turned on his attacker and fought for his life. The unexpected maneuver caught his intended executioner off guard, which was why Stabler was still alive. He had been wounded, but he had escaped. But his cunningness would not matter unless he made it to the nearest town before he bled to death.

Or the dingoes got him.

Stabler reached the bottom of the dune and ran across the open space separating him from the next hill of sand that blocked his path. Blood dripped from his wound with each step he took, leaving a trail that even the oldest and feeblest of the wild dogs could follow.

How far had he traveled now? he wondered. One mile? Two? He had no way of knowing. He knew only that somewhere between the haze of pain obscuring his vision and the continuous fire burning in his gut, his chances of living to see another outback sunrise were remarkably slim.

Everyone dies. Applegate and Curtis had. Was it his turn, too? He had to make it; he had to tell his superiors what the three men had discovered. Stabler had to let *someone* know the horrendous act that was planned. With advanced warning, perhaps the tragedy could be averted.

Stabler staggered to the crest of the dune. The muscles in his legs burned, and the ache from his wound pulsated throughout his body in ever-widening circles. But the physical pain was forgotten, and a charge of renewed strength coursed through his system when he gazed down from the top of the dune.

Below him, not more than half a mile away, were the subdued lights of a small settlement.

A dingo howled and Stabler turned. Through the darkness he could make out the silhouette of the wild dog. The beast was quickly joined by another, and another, until more than eight of the dingoes had gathered in a pack.

The feral creatures studied their prey as they paced back and forth across the dune. Several of the animals sniffed at the blood that had spilled on the sand. The scent drove them mad. The lead dingo arched his head and bayed at the star-filled sky. One by one the other wild dogs joined him. When the howling stopped, the hungry dingoes charged.

Stabler tore down the dune and raced toward the distant town. The bloodthirsty howls of the dingoes made him forget his weak legs and the steady pain of his wound. All that mattered now was that he reach the nearby settlement.

A level expanse of land ran directly to his goal. Stabler's legs were a pair of fleshy pistons. Blood from his wound leaked down along his thigh. He clamped his hand over the bullet hole and continued running. Stabler had less than a quarter mile to go.

The dingoes ran faster. Stabler could hear them racing to overtake him. He knew that their eyes would be glinting in the dark as they rushed in for the kill.

Stabler tripped over a rock. He lost and then regained his balance. The wild dogs were almost upon him. He was so close to the town. He opened his mouth to scream for help.

The wild dog leading the pack broke away from the rest and attacked. The dingo slammed into Stabler's back. Man and beast collapsed to the ground.

Jaws like steel snapped in a slavering frenzy for Stabler's throat. The man twisted, locking his hands around the dingo's neck, digging his fingers into the wild dog's fur. Stabler extended his arms, keeping the gnashing rows of teeth mere inches from his face. He exerted more pressure on his fingers as he tried to squeeze the life from the wild animal.

The second dingo attacked. Then the third. Within seconds they were all on him. One pair of jaws locked onto his shoulder, ripping away a chunk of cloth-covered meat. Another dingo tore off Stabler's right ear. Two more of the creatures launched themselves at the thrashing flesh of his ankles.

Stabler was dying; he was being devoured alive. The pain in his side was forgotten. But still he refused to release the dingo he was choking.

Stabler squeezed harder. He wished he had made it to the town. A warm mist splashed over his face, and the stars disappeared. Stabler listened to the night and smiled.

Applegate and Curtis were calling his name.

2

Hal Brognola had not been surprised by the order to meet with the President of the United States. It came with the territory. Expect the unexpected. It was the only way to remain afloat when the rest of the world was sinking.

"Good evening, Mr. President," the nation's top Federal agent said in a tired voice as he was ushered into the Oval Office.

"Good evening," the President returned. He looked even more tired than Brognola. "Have a seat, please."

Brognola took a chair across from the President's desk. He checked the time on his watch. "Do we have a problem?"

"Affirmative," the President said. "I've just received confirmation that three of our people sent to Australia on a routine investigation have vanished. The remains of one of the men was positively identified several hours ago. Apparently he was mauled to death and eaten by a pack of wild dogs."

"They're called dingoes, I believe," Brognola said.

"That's correct. A preliminary medical examination has also revealed that the victim may have sustained a single gunshot wound to the side before the dogs attacked him. The mutilated condition of the body makes it difficult to confirm that at this point."

"And the remaining two men?"

"No sign of them. If our suspicions are correct, and the known victim *was* shot prior to being attacked, then it's reasonable to assume that his two associates shared a similar fate."

"What exactly was the nature of their investigation in Australia?" the Fed inquired. "You said the investigation was routine in nature?"

"It was supposed to be. Obviously our men ruffled the feathers of the wrong bird somewhere along the line or they would still be with us. Our men were simply ordered to obtain information on Australia's Nuclear Disarmament Party. Politically, the party's still learning to crawl, but after what happened last year in New Zealand with our destroyer, the USS *Buchanan*, we can't overlook anything that might compromise our defense strategies in that region."

"Of course not," Brognola said.

The President's point was well-taken. Following a ban on nuclear-powered or nuclear-armed vessels within New Zealand's offshore limit, the Wellington government had refused to allow the USS *Buchanan* to enter its waters. The denial was prompted by the U.S.'s refusal to state whether or not the *Buchanan* was armed with nuclear weapons.

"If the New Zealand government's attitude spreads to Australia," Brognola continued, "it could effectively put an end to ANZUS."

ANZUS was the thirty-five-year-old military alliance between Australia, New Zealand and the United States.

"Right. The integrity of ANZUS must be preserved at all costs. That is why our people were looking into Australia's NDP. Frankly, the whole business has me very worried."

Brognola knew the direction the conversation was taking. This was not the first time the President had contacted him regarding an assignment involving international players. It would not likely be the last.

"You've already lost three men, sir," Brognola said, choosing his words carefully. "Perhaps it would save time, as well as further casualties, if our five specialists made a soft probe into the country? Nothing to grab the headlines. Just enough to clear the air and let us know where we stand."

"An excellent idea. The sooner we put them on this the better. And I like the idea of a soft probe. Australia is, after all, an important ally. I'd like to keep it that way. We've all enjoyed the benefits of ANZUS and should continue to do so."

"Yes, sir. I understand."

"When can we expect to have your Stony Man experts on the scene?"

"They're due to arrive here in approximately six hours. About three o'clock in the morning our time. I have them working on a brief training exercise at the moment."

"After their performance recently in Czechoslovakia, I'm surprised they would need to brush up on their skills."

"Can't have them getting rusty, sir."

The President sighed, and a tone of genuine sadness came to his voice. "That hardly seems likely considering how many times already we've had to turn to them to back us out of a tight corner."

"Mr. President, that was, after all, why they were brought together in the first place. Once they've arrived and I've briefed them on the situation, I'll get back to you."

"Do that. As soon as I know they're on their way, I'll alert the Australian Security Intelligence Organization to arrange for someone to meet them in Sydney. I'd like to see this handled as a soft probe, but I realize how quickly these missions can go wrong. With that in mind, tell your men to take all the gear they think they'll need. I'll arrange for ASIO to green light their equipment through customs."

"Very good. Is there anything else, sir?"

"Only that I want you and your men to know that you're all doing one hell of a job. I'd appreciate your passing the message along."

"I will, Mr. President," Brognola replied as he rose from the chair.

BROGNOLA MENTALLY REVIEWED his conversation with the President as he sat at his desk in the Stony Man war room. His cigar, ignored while he was deep in thought, was now little more than four inches of ash. He tapped the ash loose with the tip of his finger, then placed the butt of the smoldering stogie in his mouth.

So, Brognola thought as he savored the remains of his smoke, something underhanded was going on in Australia. The exact source of the disturbance had yet to be determined, but as director of all Stony Man operations the super Fed's confidence in Phoenix Force's ability to deal with the matter was absolute.

Located in the Blue Ridge Mountains of Virginia, the Stony Man complex had originally been organized to utilize the unique talents of Mack Bolan, the Executioner. The warrior was known throughout the world for his one-man crusade against organized crime.

Handpicked by Bolan himself, Phoenix Force was a new foreign legion, the finest freedom fighters the world could offer—five men who fought the barbarism of twentieth-century savages with the fury of five hundred.

Brognola reflected a moment longer on the past missions he had helped to coordinate and then turned his attention to the future. Phoenix Force would go to Australia. Stony Man's crack antiterrorist team would embark once more on a mission whose outcome would be measured by the courage and dogged determination of the Force's five commandos.

The Fed checked the time and then set to work. Phoenix Force would leave for the southern continent as soon as their training exercise in Florida was completed.

Silently, Brognola wished his warriors well.

3

The grass airstrip was only as long as it needed to be. Thick vegetation surrounded it on three sides. Overhead, a full moon provided a degree of natural lighting for the runway. The setting was engulfed in the stillness of the August night that was broken only by the armies of insects that swarmed and buzzed through the humid air.

A narrow road, little more than twin dirt tracks gouged from the soil, led to the start of the makeshift landing strip. Two vehicles, with their headlights off and using the reflected light of the moon to guide them, slowly traveled over the uneven surface of the path. The lead vehicle was a late-model station wagon with squeaking shocks. Following behind was a Chevrolet van.

The estate car came to a halt ten feet from the strip. The van stopped inches short of the station wagon's rear bumper. The engine of each vehicle was turned off. Doors popped open, and the occupants got out.

The station wagon carried six passengers; the van's riders numbered seven. All were male and all were armed. Two of the thirteen toted shotguns.

Someone barked out a terse command in Spanish, and the men quickly began to clear the landing site of debris. They worked quietly while the pair with the shotguns stood guard.

The sentries were attuned to the sounds and sights of the night. Something splashed into the water of a nearby marsh. The guards were not alarmed. With fingers caressing the triggers of their weapons, the two men calmly watched and waited as the runway was cleared. A mosquito landed on one of the men's forearms and was crushed by the slap of an open palm.

Less than ten feet away an unseen audience enjoyed the show. Hidden by the teeming plant life that bordered the landing strip, the five commandos blended in with the luscious vegetation.

Nearest to the sentries, his stomach pressed to the ground, was Colonel Yakov Katzenelenbogen. Clutched in the fingers of his left hand was an Uzi 9 mm SMG.

Katz served as the unit commander of Phoenix Force. His credentials as an expert in combat, espionage and intelligence, and antiterrorist tactics were impeccable. The son of Russian Jews who immigrated to France after the Bolshevik Revolution, Yakov's linguistically talented father raised the boy to speak fluent English, Russian, French and German.

After his family became victims of Hitler's Nazi tyranny, the orphaned lad joined the underground resistance movement. He was later recruited by the American OSS to penetrate enemy lines, where he perfected his skills of clandestine sabotage and urban warfare. Following World War II, Katz participated with the Haganah in Palestine and fought for the State of Israel's independence.

He lost his only son, and his right arm, in an explosion during the Six Day War. Katz refused to dwell on past misfortunes, however, and soon became a top agent in Mossad, Israel's major espionage and intelligence organization. In that capacity he found himself rubbing elbows with the American CIA, the British SIS, the French Sûreté, as well as the West German BND.

Physically, with his iron-gray hair, serene blue eyes and slightly paunchy midsection, the one-armed soldier looked more like a college professor. His appearance was deceiving, a sobering fact that scores of the Israeli commando's enemies had learned the hard way.

Next to Katzenelenbogen, and also concealed by the dense foliage surrounding the landing strip, was Gary Manning, the Canadian representative on the Phoenix Force team. Ruggedly handsome and built like lumberjacks are supposed to be, Manning was one of the world's foremost demolition experts. His friends bragged that the Canadian could blow the whipped cream off an ice-cream sundae without disturbing the cherry on top.

Manning's abilities went beyond his expertise with explosives. He was also the Phoenix squad's best rifle marksman. His early combat training included his role as an observer with the Special Forces in Vietnam. His performance in the Vietnamese hellground earned him the Silver Star. Manning was one of the few Canadian citizens to receive this decoration.

Returning to his homeland, Manning was recruited into the intelligence division of the Royal Canadian Mounted Police. Through a reciprocal exchange program with West Germany, the barrel-chested powerhouse was transferred to Europe where he served with the newly created GSG-9, the Federal Republic of Germany's elite counterterrorist unit.

After the RCMP folded its intelligence operation, Manning was recalled and offered a secure position that would have tied him to a desk for the rest of his professional career. Manning's response to the offer was a two-word reply that soon had the Canadian working in the private sector.

A brief marriage was dissolved before all of the thank-you notes were mailed. Manning shrugged the divorce off and concentrated on business. His persistence paid off when he was hired as a highly paid security consultant and junior executive of North American International, a position he held when he was approached to become one of Phoenix Force's founding members. Manning did not have to be asked twice.

As he watched the men from the station wagon and the van work their way to the end of the runway, Manning maintained a firm grip on his Anschutz airgun, one of the finest air rifles in use. Powered by a CO_2 cartridge, and fitted with an infrared scope similar to a Starlite scanner, the Anschutz fired steel darts coated with a Valium solution, Thorazine or a specified poison of Manning's choosing. In Manning's hands the Anschutz could single out a target in seconds.

"¡Mierda!" the shotgunner in front of Manning swore, swatting another of the voracious insects swarming about him.

Such language, Calvin James thought as the Colombian swore again. Nestled well off the landing strip behind a clump of palmettos, Calvin James cradled his Ring Airfoil grenade launcher and sat perfectly still.

Born and reared on Chicago's tough south side, James had the distinction of being the youngest Phoenix Force member. Enlisting in the navy when he was seventeen, he trained long and hard as a hospital corpsman. His dedication to duty served him well and eventually brought him to the attention of the SEALs. This, in turn, lead to a two-year stint with a special operations group in Vietnam. James was wounded during his final SOG mission and returned to the U.S. with an honorable discharge and a medal for bravery.

Calvin James's homecoming predicated a numbing series of personal family tragedies including the murders of his mother and sister. He had just started to study medicine and chemistry at UCLA on the G.I. Bill, but after attending his sister's funeral James scrapped his dual majors in favor of an education in police science. He subsequently joined the San Francisco Police Department, and later became an important member of that city's SWAT team, a position he held when first approached by Phoenix Force.

What he may have lacked in years, the tall, lanky black man from Chicago more than made up for with experience. Calvin James was a dynamo in combat, a man whose contribution to the Stony Man supersquad could not be measured in mere words of praise.

Across from Calvin James, and hiding inside the wall of vegetation on the opposite side of the makeshift runway, were the final two men currently answering the Phoenix Force roll call—Karl Hahn and David McCarter.

An agent with the West German BND, that nation's federal intelligence service, Hahn's first introduction to Phoenix Force came when he assisted the team on a mission to thwart a KGB plot in Turkey. When Rafael Encizo, the Cuban-born member of the elite fighting unit, became disabled during a furious clash with ODESSA Nazis in the south of France, Phoenix Force was left one man short. Karl Hahn was invited to fill the void for as long as necessary.

A muscular man in his mid-thirties, Hahn attended high school in southern California on a student exchange program and later majored in computer programming at UCLA. He was fluent in German, English and Turkish, and could make himself understood in Czech, Russian and French if his life depended on it.

Before signing on with the BND, Hahn had served with GSG-9. During his time with them he participated in many key antiterrorist strikes, including those made against the Baader-Meinhof gang, the German Red Army and Turkish terrorists operating out of

West Berlin. Hahn's transfer to the BND came about after he waged a one-man vendetta against the Red Army. His hatred for this group grew after a close GSG-9 friend was tortured, castrated and blinded by the Red Army monsters.

In addition to his other talents, Karl Hahn was also an electronics wizard and an expert in weapons design; both were skills that Phoenix Force relied upon with confidence. As he waited now for the final participant of the evening's drama to arrive, Hahn pulled his H&K MP-5 submachine gun tighter to his body. He was anxious for Hal Brognola's training exercise to begin.

Beside Hahn, and with an Ingram MAC-10 resting across his lap, was David McCarter. The British commando had been a member of Phoenix Force since its inception. A true Cockney, born within the sound of Bow bells in London's East End, the fox-faced McCarter was one of a kind.

David McCarter believed in jamming as much excitement into one's life as possible. A veteran of Great Britain's Strategic Air Service, he was also a former national champion of the British pistol marksmanship team.

A master of virtually every form of combat and an excellent pilot, the sometimes verbally caustic Englishman had seen action in Southeast Asia, had been stationed in Oman during the Omani Ohofar War, had gone undercover for two years and had infiltrated the cells of Communist subversives active in Hong Kong and had participated in the decisive SAS raid on the Iranian embassy in London in 1980.

McCarter thrived on danger and often set the pace for the offensive measures that Phoenix Force engaged in. With a tendency to be moody and impatient prior to battle, the British commando had almost reached the limits of his patience when the first sounds of an aircraft reached his ears. McCarter grinned and felt at peace with himself. His wait was over.

The men clearing the landing strip had also heard the approaching airplane. Together they hurried back to the start of the runway where they separated and took up positions on either side of the strip. Each of the gun-wielding smugglers stood approximately three feet apart.

One of the guards joined the group on his right so that the number of men on each side of the runway was even. The second guard draped his shotgun in the crook of his arm and crossed to the driver's side of the station wagon.

The drone of the aircraft's engine was getting much louder when the man at the station wagon reached through the window and pulled on the vehicle's headlights. Simultaneously, the remaining twelve men produced miniature high-intensity krypton bulb flashlights; the combined effect of their efforts served to illuminate the area where the landing strip began.

Moments later the plane swooped out of the sky just above the station wagon. It dropped and made a relatively smooth landing on the dirt-and-grass runway. Bouncing and rolling over the bumpy terrain, the single-prop plane slowed as it traveled to the end of the strip. The men had also cleared a circular section of land to enable the pilot to turn the craft around and head it back in the direction of the waiting men. Halfway back up the runway, the pilot brought the three-hundred-horsepower Cessna to a halt. The prop stopped turning, and the pilot left the cockpit and jumped from the plane.

The lights of the automobile went dark. So did the dozen krypton bulb flashlights. The bright moon lit the scene in a silvery glow as all but the two guards carrying the shotguns rushed toward the Cessna to begin unloading the precious cargo. Hal Brognola had assured Phoenix Force that the incoming shipment would be pure cocaine, and once again Brognola's sources had come through.

As Phoenix Force watched, one of the Colombians leaped inside the single-engine workhorse and began passing out duffel bags to his friends. Gary Manning observed all of this through the infrared scope of his Anschutz, then directed his aim and attention to the soft exposed flesh of the pilot's throat. The last thing the Stony Man soldiers wanted to deal with was a runaway plane.

Manning's finger curled around the airgun's trigger and squeezed. His unerring aim sent the Anschutz's Thorazine-filled steel dart straight into its intended target. The pilot emitted a sharp intake of breath, then fell to the dirt as if his legs had been kicked from under him. The drug-dazed sky jockey lay motionless on the ground as though dead.

"¡Coño!" one of the Colombians shouted as he and the others rushed to the pilot.

Both shotgunners deserted their posts to see what all the excitement was about. The sentries got more than they bargained for as Calvin James suddenly rose to his feet and whistled. The guards stopped and turned toward the noise.

"¡Adelante," James shouted, his Ring Airfoil grenade launcher held at the ready.

Everyone on the makeshift airstrip turned toward the Phoenix fighter's voice. One smuggler dealt with the black American's unexpected appearance by bringing his assault rifle around to bear on James.

David McCarter, deciding to even the odds, aimed his Ingram MAC-10 and opened fire with a three-round burst. The volley lasted less than a second. The bullets punched across the would-be killer's midsection, exposing his organs to the air. The gunman screamed, flung his rifle aside and then sank to his knees in a fit of dark pain.

The sentry nearest Phoenix Force managed to aim his Remington Model 870 in their direction just as cross fire from Yakov Katzenelenbogen and Karl Hahn cut the man down. Splinters flew from the 870's American walnut stock as a hailstorm of lead-lined fury reduced the gun's owner to a raw and writhing piece of flesh. The doomed guard collapsed over the stock of his shattered Remington and died.

Guard number two wielded a Winchester Defender, but the shotgun was about as useful as a toy gun with a cork jammed up its barrel. Having traded his Anschutz for an Eagle .357 Magnum, Manning stopped the second sentry for a brief heart-to-heart. The brawny Canadian's .357 did all of the talking.

Twice Manning's Desert Eagle boomed, each shot striking the guard's breastbone. The sternum cracked apart. Ribs became jagged shards and punctured both lungs. A bubble of blood filled the man's mouth and burst from his lips.

Karl Hahn's next encounter with the enemy came when a Colombian discarded his duffel bag and brought the submachine gun that was slung over his shoulder into play. The smuggler's fingers closed over his weapon as the duffel bag of cocaine hit the dirt.

Hahn opened fire with his H&K MP-5 and promptly assisted the drug runner in making an important career decision. The West German's H&K voted for early retirement.

Three 9 mm parabellum bullets chopped into the hood's abdomen. Blood spurted from the triple assault. Another slug from Hahn's machine pistol struck the subgunner in the wrist, breaking the ulna in two as if the bone were a breadstick. The wounded man inhaled, and massive shock stopped his heart forever.

Less than one minute had elapsed since the beginning of the battle. One of the drug runners broke away from his partners and unleashed a blinding sweep of lead with his SMG. Most of the Phoenix Force team dived for safety. Calvin James did not. Before the Colombian could zero in on the black commando's position, James flexed his finger against the RAG's trigger and sent one of the weapon's doughnut-shaped projectiles straight into a head-on collision with the Cessna's propeller blades.

The 53 mm airfoil round impacted and exploded. So did the Cessna. With its pilot and copilot seats modified to contain extra fuel, the single-engine plane erupted into a ball of churning smoke and flame. Another shot from the RAG launcher plowed into the burning wreckage and set off a secondary explosion.

The Colombian who had been passing out the duffel bags from the Cessna was killed instantly, bathed in a fiery wash of fuel and shrapnel that squeezed the life from his body. The propeller separated from the front of the plane and went spinning into the crowd of Colombian gunmen.

Two of the smugglers were decapitated by the whirling blades. Another had his left arm removed at the shoulder. The propeller completed its mission by impaling a forth man through the stomach, pinning him to the surface of the landing strip as if he were a mounted insect.

The killer trying to zap James gave up when he and two of his friends were showered by petrol. One by one the three men ignited in a roaring rush of flame. The bright orange fireballs screamed and danced over the body of the Cessna's unconscious pilot as fire consumed their flesh. McCarter hosed the trio down with a volley of mercy rounds from his Ingram.

Only one of the Colombian drug hustlers had escaped the carnage unscathed. Surrounded by flames, the lone survivor of the original thirteen smugglers frantically emptied the magazine of his S&W M-469 at both real and imaginary targets.

Two of the autoloader's 9 mm Luger slugs popped through the station wagon's windshield, spiderwebbing the safety glass from end to end. The Chevrolet van behind it suffered a similar fate. Another couple of bullets crashed into the station wagon's radiator. The desperate gunman even tried to knock the moon out of the sky. Then the M-469's magazine ran dry and the drug runner attempted to reload.

"Not this time, junior," Manning said, and promptly brought the gunman down with a single shot from his Eagle.

The Colombian dropped his weapon to clasp his hands to his chest and then slowly corkscrewed dead to the ground.

Flames devoured the grass runway. A cloud of smoke threatened to eclipse the moon. Nothing was left of the Cessna or the duffel bags filled with cocaine.

"Looks like we broke up their party," James said.

"Right," McCarter agreed. "Busted it right off the bloody map."

4

"The DEA ran into the results of your training exercise shortly after you flew out of Miami," Hal Brognola informed Phoenix Force.

"How are they taking it?" asked Manning. "Upset, I'll bet."

"That's putting it politely," Brognola confirmed. "The DEA is pissed off. Its agents consider the entire state of Florida their ballpark. They don't like the fact that outsiders were able to roust a big drug deal before they had a chance to intervene. The DEA is calling in a lot of favors in an effort to find out who you guys are. It's not the bust they mind so much, but the fact that they weren't invited along for the ride."

"I bet they're not half as upset as the men who financed the delivery of the cocaine," Hahn concluded. "When the coke and the men who were sent to retrieve it both fail to materialize, heads are going to roll somewhere down the line."

"Seems to me they already have," McCarter said, recalling the damage wreaked by the flying propeller blade. "But enough about the great job we did in the

Sunshine State. I don't know about the rest of you gents, but this old Cockney's knackered."

"You'll get plenty of rest later," Brognola promised. "The flight from New York to Sydney is a long one."

"Sydney?" McCarter repeated. "What's going on in the land down under?"

"That's what I'm sending the five of you to Australia to find out," Brognola said.

Katz frowned. "Trouble?"

Brognola nodded. "While you were in Florida last night I had a chat with the President."

"I don't suppose you mentioned my tax refund?" James inquired. "I should have gotten it six months ago, man."

"What did the President have to say?" Katz inquired. "If he's involved, why hasn't the media picked up on it by now?"

"Forget the newshounds," Brognola responded. "They don't know anything about this, and that's the way we want to keep it."

Hal Brognola spent the next five minutes relating the details of his conversation with the President. "That's the extent of what we know at this time," he told his men. "One Company man is confirmed dead. According to the report I received, the man was attacked and eaten by a pack of dingoes. Before he was killed the victim may also have sustained a single gunshot wound to the side. You should have a definite on that when you touch down in Sydney."

"What about the agent's two friends?" Hahn asked.

Brognola shook his head. "We're not holding much hope. It's assumed both men are dead."

"And all because they were investigating this Nuclear Disarmament Party?" James questioned. "What do we have on the group?"

"Not a great deal," Brognola answered. "They're an emerging political party whose platform calls for Australia to ban nuclear-based weaponry on the continent."

"I know that the NDP is a relatively small organization," McCarter said, "but they do have their share of supporters. Last year an antinuclear activist, the leader of a popular rock group, ran on the NDP ticket and squared off against the Australian prime minister in a televised debate. The NDP candidate didn't win the election, but the margin between the two parties was narrow enough to leave the traditional politicos very shaken."

"The President's concern is understandable," Manning said. "If the Australian government decides to go the antinuke route, it would make the ANZUS alliance useless."

"Which would tickle the Reds pink," James decided. "With ANZUS destroyed, the Communists might be tempted to expand their sphere of influence in the region."

"Precisely," Brognola concurred. "Which is the reason your mission to Australia is essential. The

Communists gain enough ground as it is without us making it easy for them.''

Katz motioned to Brognola. "Will we be covering this one blind, Hal? Or has an assist been arranged in advance for us?"

"The President assured me that you would have the full cooperation of ASIO. Just before your arrival I received verification that your contact will be an agent named Blake. Agent Blake will meet your flight at Kingsford Smith Airport."

"Does that mean the ASIO is going to be looking over our shoulders the whole time we're there?" McCarter asked, already anticipating problems. "If we have to hold hands with them every step of the way, we'll never get anything done."

"ASIO has been instructed to help you in any way possible," Brognola countered. "No more, no less. Their agents won't like it, but if they *do* get in your way, then it's up to you to politely tell them to butt out."

"If it comes to that," Manning suggested, casting a wary eye at McCarter, "then I'd better be the one to tell them. It doesn't take much to launch an international incident, and I'm sure David would find a way to accomplish the task with ease."

"Not me," McCarter protested. "I'm a true diplomat."

Manning shrugged and smiled at his friend. "You'll have to show me the dictionary you use sometime."

"Gary has a point," Brognola said. "The President and I have agreed that this venture into Australian territory should be treated strictly as a soft probe. Neither one of us wants to see you featured on the evening news.

"If things do heat up, however, you'll have access to any equipment you elect to take into the country with you. Clearance with Australian customs will be overseen by your ASIO contact."

"How much does ASIO know about us?" Hahn asked.

"Not enough to put on a postcard," Brognola replied. "As far as they're concerned, the five of you are a multinational troubleshooting team hired by the United States government to look into this business concerning the three Company men."

"Fair enough," Katz said. "What about cover names?"

"I'll leave that up to you," Brognola said. "ASIO only has a very sketchy physical description of each of you. None of your names have been supplied."

"That's how we prefer it," Katz said as he got to his feet. "It'll be light soon. What time does our flight leave Kennedy?"

Brognola told him.

"Then we'd better start packing," the Israeli colonel continued. "Is there anything else?"

The rest of Phoenix Force rose as Hal Brognola answered. "Good luck," he told his men. "I have a feeling that you're going to need it."

5

Everyone agreed that Sebastian Hardy looked like Orson Welles.... Hardy was overweight. He knew it. So did anyone else who came in contact with the man.

"If Sebastian gets any bigger, they'll be able to track him by radar," a young boy joked to his classmates when Hardy was only twelve.

Even the schoolteacher got a chuckle out of that one.

When Hardy entered college, his weight problem and the inevitable remarks that accompanied it went with him. Nor were the comments regarding his obese condition limited to verbal abuse.

In a safe-deposit box at one of the three Australian banks in which he held a controlling interest, Hardy still kept a copy of a university newspaper dated more than twenty years before. Featured at the top of the paper's humor page was the question: How does Sebastian Hardy iron his clothes? The answer: He puts them on.

Sebastian Hardy kept the painful memento to constantly remind himself of how viciously cruel his fellow human beings could be. Not that he had any trouble remembering all of the witty remarks he had inspired down through the years. Every malicious comment made regarding his obesity was burned into his memory.

Hardy quit school the day he inherited a million pounds from an uncle in England. His parents were outraged that they were ignored in the will, but Hardy had only laughed and refused their request to share in his newfound wealth. Hardy's mother and father had always been embarrassed by their son's chronic weight problem and had often gone to great lengths to ensure Sebastian's absence from important social functions.

Inheriting such a substantial sum from his late uncle's estate changed everything. For the first time in his life Hardy was able to enjoy the benefits of total independence. He no longer needed his parents' financial support. He had always lived without their love; now he could afford to live without their money.

Through a series of shrewd real estate transactions, Hardy parlayed his inheritance into holdings worth millions more. He possessed an uncanny talent for recognizing potential sources of income well before any of his contemporaries. His was the touch of Midas. All business deals catching his interest soon yielded golden profits.

When uranium deposits were discovered on a parcel of land Hardy owned, he kept the news of the find under wraps and quickly secured the deeds to every piece of property within a twenty-mile radius. Before he was through, Hardy had purchased enough land on which to build a city.

Subsequent excavations revealed that Hardy's uranium deposits were among the largest in the continent's history. A full-scale mining operation was quickly developed to extract the radioactive element.

Mining the uranium was one thing, but finding buyers for the rare element was something else entirely. The United States dominated the extremely limited world uranium market.

In an effort to combat the U.S. Atomic Energy Commission's virtual monopoly on uranium production and sales, several producers throughout the world had formed a defensive cartel. Designed to allocate quotas and to set world uranium prices, the cartel originally had no intention of including Australia as a partner.

With his entire fortune riding on the success or failure of his uranium mining venture, however, Sebastian Hardy had no option but to force his way into what later became known as the Club of Five. The group included France, Canada, South Africa and Britain, and finally Australia.

Hardy's initiation into the Club of Five took place in May of 1972. The financially astute businessman had not looked back. In the years following his association with the Club, Hardy had amassed a net worth greater than most emerging Third World nations. His accountants maintained that Sebastian Hardy was invincible.

Hardy, shoveling a spoonful of rich chocolate mousse into his mouth, knew that his accountants were wrong. He may have ranked as one of the world's wealthiest men, but that counted for nothing given the uneasy tenor of the times. The globe was teetering on the brink of disaster, total annihilation. The super-powers were playing nuclear roulette, and the future of humanity hung in the balance. If Hardy survived a nuclear war, he doubted that his money—and the gourmet delights he could buy with that money—would have any value in a world of mutants and wastelands.

Unless something monumentally bold and fantastic was done to avert the inevitable, Hardy believed that life on earth was doomed. Hardy was torn. He lived the high life off the success of the very element that would ultimately destroy it all. Hardy knew there had to be a way around the situation, and one evening while feasting on a plate of Rouen duckling with truffles the big man concocted his plan.

He dubbed his scheme for world salvation Operation Thor. The title was apt. Thor was the ancient Norse god of thunder. If Hardy and his compatriots were successful, the thunder they were about to create would set the pronuclear movement back more than a hundred years. Once again the world would be subjected to the destructive force of a nuclear bomb.

But Sebastian Hardy also wanted to promote his belief that uranium should continue to be used in the production of nuclear power. It was, after all, his meal ticket. He only wanted the major powers to cease the production of nuclear arms. With the advent of Australia's Nuclear Disarmament Party, Hardy was able to recruit a number of influential visionaries like himself. Unfortunately, while the NDP's political aspirations were admirable, good intentions would not get a job done. By the time the NDP achieved enough clout to make any difference, Australia and the rest of the global community would be reduced to nothing more than a charred cinder of atomic rubble.

And so Hardy formed the Nuclear Free Australia party. Now, sitting at the head of his conference table in a plush, cushioned chair especially designed to comfortably support his enormous girth, Sebastian Hardy realized that his original inspiration for Operation Thor had been a stroke of genius. It was because of that genius that the planet would be spared a nuclear nightmare, and that his bank account would continue to increase from the sale of uranium.

Joining Hardy at the conference room table were nine other people. Eight men and one woman. All but two were native Australians; Douglas Rice and Sheryl Galloway had been invited by Hardy to participate in the NFA because they had been instrumental in the launch of a similar antinuclear program in their homeland of New Zealand.

Hardy scraped the final traces of mousse from the bottom of his bowl and licked his spoon shiny clean. He took a sip of chilled mineral water and then deftly removed the plastic wrapper from a piece of peppermint candy that was as wide and as long as his thumb.

"This meeting," he announced as he fed the peppermint into his mouth, "will now come to order." Hardy nodded to the smartly dressed man seated on his right. "What about the minutes from last week's get-together, Cheswick?"

Lawrence Cheswick snapped open the notebook in front of him. "Not much on that account, Sebastian. We discussed what measures to take regarding the three Americans who were asking the questions about the NDP." Cheswick glanced up from his notes. "As you may recall, the meeting finished early."

"I remember," Hardy said. "I wanted to be the first in line for the grand opening of that new Chinese restaurant—The Dragon Inn—but take my advice and don't bother trying it. The boofheads don't know an egg roll from a bread roll."

"Sorry to hear that, Sebastian," Cheswick said on behalf of the others.

Hardy shrugged and crunched the piece of candy between his molars as he reached for another. "Never mind. I could have been their best customer, but they blew it. Where were we?"

"Talking about the Americans investigating the NDP," Cheswick answered.

"That's right," Hardy agreed. "We've insulated ourselves too well to be linked with the Nuclear Disarmament Party. Most of the NDP's supporters are completely unaware that our Nuclear Free Australia movement exists. Nevertheless, with Operation Thor virtually upon us, we cannot take any chances. Do we have an update available?"

A thin bean pole of a man who slouched in his seat raised a finger.

Hardy acknowledged the man. "Thompson?"

Ronald Thompson adjusted his slouch, then ran his finger inside and around the too-tight collar of his shirt. The timid man was uncomfortable with what he had to report. "Sebastian, all three of the Americans have been disposed of. Our Darwin people lured them into the outback where Bromly took care of them."

"Splendid," Hardy said. "And the method Mr. Bromly used for their executions?"

"Two of the Americans were eliminated with gunshot wounds to the head. Each was a clean kill."

"And the third American?"

Thompson's scrawny face clouded over. "The fellow turned on Bromly before our man could put him away properly."

Hardy used his tongue to tuck his second peppermint into the side of his cheek. "Go on."

"Bromly said the third American kicked him one in the face and then took off into the dunes."

"The American got away then?" Hardy inquired.

"Not by a long shot," the man named Thompson replied, "which is what Bromly nailed the American with just before he disappeared into the night. Bromly swears he plugged the bloke with a ripper in the gut."

"I assume Bromly followed our quarry?" Hardy asked.

"He did, but he lost him in the mulga," Thompson reported.

"Then it would appear that we still have a problem," Hardy said.

Thompson shook his head. "Not exactly, Sebastian. Bromly may have lost the American, but the dingoes didn't. They must have caught the scent of the blood dripping from his wound and chased the beggar down. Caught up to him just before he could make good his escape. Not much left but bones and scraps after they were through with him."

Hardy crunched his peppermint to bits and swallowed. "I'm pleased to hear that. Mr. Bromly will have to be reprimanded for his carelessness, of course, but the matter regarding the Americans, it seems, has been taken care of. Did the Americans reveal who they were working for?"

Thompson toyed with the collar of his shirt again and replied. "The Americans didn't tell Bromly a thing. Sebastian . . . was it really necessary to kill them?"

Hardy momentarily ignored Thompson's question as he leaned over and flipped open an insulated cooler beside his chair. He removed a raspberry-flavored ice block. As there were only five of the Australian popsicles left, he saw no reason to share the frozen treats with the others. Besides, he convinced himself as he unwrapped the ice block, raspberry was not a very popular flavor.

"I should have you shot for that remark. No one will stand in our way. Is it not better to sacrifice a few lives in order to save millions including, and most importantly, ourselves?'' Hardy demanded. ''Those men had to be CIA.''

''Fat lot of good it did them,'' Thompson spoke without thinking, and immediately wanted to crawl into a corner and hide. ''I'm...that is...so sorry, Sebastian,'' he stammered. ''Absolutely no offense intended. None at all.''

''And no offense taken.'' Hardy smiled, biting off the end of his ice block. ''You're correct about the Americans, though. Their association with the CIA didn't help them at all. How much did the Americans learn before they were terminated?''

''Whatever it was,'' Thompson was fast to point out, ''it wasn't enough to jeopardize Operation Thor. Any information they might have relayed to their superiors will not affect our plans. We're completely in the clear.''

''Unless the Americans send someone else to determine what became of the three men they lost,'' Sheryl Galloway suggested. She was one of the two NFA members from New Zealand. ''I imagine that the disappearance of three of their agents will rouse some kind of reaction from the United States.''

''Let the Yanks send all the people they want,'' Hardy said. ''They'll get the same reception their predecessors received. Our timetable for Operation Thor is precise. For Thor to be the total success we know is possible, there can be no deviation from our schedule. In a few more hours the countdown will begin.

"The Americans will not be a problem," Hardy continued, assuring everyone at the conference table. "In anticipation of further CIA interference, I have all available local NFA personnel scouring Sydney for further signs of an American presence here. If and when more Yanks arrive, they will be dealt with immediately. In the meantime, let's let them speculate about the fate of their three men. By the time the Americans realize what we have set out to do, they will be reading about Operation Thor in their history books."

Hardy slurped the stick of his ice block dry. "Who's staying for lunch?"

6

Calvin James looked out the window of the Pan American jumbo 747 and yawned.

"Wonderful," he commented quietly to McCarter who was seated next to him. "We fly halfway around the world, sit through two cinematic sleepers disguised as entertainment, tie on the feed bag for five TV dinners and a couple of snacks, and on top of everything else lose a whole day in the process because we had to travel across so many time zones to get to Sydney...and what do they do once we land?"

McCarter glanced out the window over James's shoulder and took a wild guess. "Looks like they're giving our jet a bit of a wash."

"Looks like that to me, too," James agreed.

Gary Manning leaned over from the row of seats behind them. "Australia imposes strict controls on the importation of food, animals, plants and their by-products," he informed the pair. "All international flights are sprayed down to disinfect them before any passengers are permitted to disembark."

McCarter turned around in his seat. "What have you been up to then? Moonlighting as an Aussie tour guide on the sly?"

"I hit Sydney for R & R back in the sixties," the Canadian explained. "Some things don't change."

The jumbo's intercom came on. An air hostess thanked the passengers for their patience and announced that deplaning would begin immediately. A senior citizens' group sitting in the rear of the jet cheered when they heard the news.

Yakov Katzenelenbogen, sitting next to Karl Hahn in the 747's forward cabin, wanted to let loose with a little cheering himself. With a stronger aversion to flying than McCarter's for unwrinkled clothes, the Israeli colonel was only too happy to finally be leaving the plane.

"Long flight," Hahn remarked.

Katz unbuckled his seat belt. "I know. And lucky us, we get to do it all over again when it's time to go home."

By prior arrangement Katz was to be the first of the Phoenix Force team to leave the plane. Blake, the ASIO agent they were supposed to meet, had been given a brief description of the Israeli commando. Once Katz and Blake established contact, the remaining four members of the Stony Man squad would join them. They would then be cleared through customs and leave with Blake for downtown Sydney.

Katz stood, then stepped into the aisle. He and Hahn had flown first class, and therefore he would be one of the first passengers to exit the aircraft. Although the line moved slowly, Katz soon found himself exiting through the forward door and following his fellow passengers as they made their way to customs. Despite the claustrophobic atmosphere generated by the crowds, Katz was still very relieved to be back on the ground once again.

Katz made it to the luggage arrival area designated for his flight just as an assortment of suitcases, boxes and the occasional footlocker started to spill onto a revolving metal conveyance. Phoenix Force had been among the final passengers boarding the jumbo jet in New York, which meant their luggage had been part of the last to be packed in the 747's baggage compartment.

Last on . . . first off, Katz thought, and was pleased that less than thirty seconds later his suitcase and sports bag appeared. He hoisted the suitcase from the moving conveyance with his left hand and claimed the handles of his gym bag with the three-pronged hook of the prosthesis he wore attached to his right arm.

"Mr. Wayne?" a voice addressed Katz by the Phoenix commander's cover name.

The Israeli turned to the sound of the voice. "Yes, I'm . . ." He halted in midsentence. "You're Blake?"

The woman flashed Katz an honest smile and nodded. "You've got it. Pleased to meet you."

Katz placed his luggage on the floor and accepted the woman's hand. Her grip was firm.

"A pleasure to meet *you*," the Israeli countered. "The others should be along any minute."

Agent Blake's physical attributes belied the true nature of her chosen profession. With a statuesque build, honey-blond hair that fell in a perfect wave over her shoulders and brilliant blue eyes, Phoenix Force's ASIO contact could easily have graced the covers of a dozen famous glamour magazines.

Dressed stylishly in black leather shoes, a calf-length wraparound skirt with matching jacket and a cream-colored blouse that accentuated the fullness of her figure, Agent Blake smiled warmly at Katz.

"I'm not exactly what you expected," Blake guessed.

"I'm not complaining," Katz said.

Hahn emerged from the Pan Am flight at that moment and crossed to where Katz and their ASIO contact were standing. The West German's initial reaction to Agent Blake did not vary greatly from his colleague's. Katz introduced the two, using Hahn's cover name of Frobe, and continued the introductions after James and McCarter joined the group. Agent Blake was shaking hands with McCarter when Manning suddenly appeared.

The ASIO agent's smile grew warmer when she saw the Canadian for the first time. She dropped McCarter's hand and threw her arms around an astonished Manning.

"Was it my breath?" McCarter asked, commenting to James and looking at his empty hand.

While the others watched the obvious display of affection, Agent Blake broke her embrace with Manning and said, "Hello, Gary."

A still surprised Manning said back, "Hello, Lila."

"Lila Blake," the ASIO woman told him.

Manning exchanged glances with his friends from Stony Man, then slowly replied, "No kidding."

7

Rafael Encizo completed his regimen of one hundred sit-ups and rose in a single graceful movement from the inclined exercise board. Sweat sheened the Cuban's body as he crossed the room and adjusted the weights on the leg lift machine to seventy-five pounds. Encizo wiped his face dry with a towel, then climbed onto the machine to continue his workout.

The clock on the wall said it was 2:15 in the morning. The Cuban had the physical therapy room of the U.S. Army hospital in Nuremberg, Germany, to himself. Not even the warm air circulating through the metal ducts near the ceiling disturbed his thoughts as he concentrated on doing his leg lifts. First the right, then the left, extending each leg straight out to the mental count of five, before lowering it and switching to the opposite leg.

Back and forth he worked. After several minutes of this, he proceeded to raise and lower his limbs in a swinging motion. The Cuban's muscles ached, but he ignored the discomfort. The pain told him he was alive and served as a potent reminder of how fortunate he was to be feeling anything at all.

Rafael Encizo had not intended to become part of a successful counterterrorist unit, yet from the very beginning the handsome Cuban's contributions were a definite asset to the Stony Man team. A veteran of the Bay of Pigs invasion, Encizo was captured by the Communists and sentenced to life in the infamous El Principe, the home away from home Castro generously provided for his political adversaries.

Beaten and starved, Encizo was subjected to a rigorous reeducation program supervised by skilled Soviet "technicians." Their job was to torture the rebellious Rafael until he conformed to their way of thinking. Much to his captor's dismay, Encizo proved to be an easy convert to the reconditioning process. This apparent conversion lasted long enough for prison officials to relax their vigilance and to get careless. One broken neck and a dead guard later, the "reformed" Encizo succeeded in making a daring escape.

Encizo became a naturalized citizen upon returning to the United States. He found work as a treasure hunter, professional bodyguard and scuba instructor before landing a job as an insurance investigator specializing in maritime claims.

Loyal to his friends, and deadly as a cobra when dealing with his opponents, the stocky Cuban had fought alongside his Phoenix Force teammates on more than twenty missions before his adventurous past caught up with him. The skull fracture and concussion he sustained during a clash with ODESSA Nazis in France had almost killed him, but Encizo was now confident that his wounds were sufficiently healed to allow him to rejoin Phoenix Force on a full-time basis.

Katz and the others had already participated on three missions that he knew of without him. Although he realized that Karl Hahn had been an ideal choice to temporarily fill the manpower gap created by his absence, Encizo also knew that he would never be truly satisfied with himself until he was permanently reunited with his Stony Man friends.

"Couldn't sleep?"

Encizo stopped doing his leg lifts when Colonel Towers entered the room. It was the doc's expertise with a scalpel that had saved Encizo's life on the operating table when he was first brought to the hospital.

"Feeling restless," Encizo told the surgeon. "The inactivity in this place gets to you after a while."

The middle-aged, slightly balding doctor laughed. "You should catch it from my end some time."

"No thanks, Doctor. Nothing personal, but I've seen all of your hospital that I want to."

"I understand. You're anxious to leave."

"Can you blame me?"

Towers, who was convinced that Encizo was involved with the CIA, shook his head. "Of course not. But I didn't put you back together just to have you run out of here and get yourself killed."

"True. But you didn't patch me up so I could spend the rest of my life catching dust, either, Doc. You have your road to follow. I have mine. The fact is, I'm about as recovered as I'm going to be. It's time to move on. You know it. So do I. What do you say you release me in the morning so I can get back to work?''

"When I think you're ready,'' Towers promised.

"And when's that going to be?'' Encizo asked.

"When I think you're ready,'' the doctor repeated.

8

"I take it you two know each other," David McCarter remarked, referring to Gary Manning and Lila Blake.

"Managed to figure that all out by yourself, huh?" Calvin James remarked dryly.

Phoenix Force had collected their baggage and were pushing the luggage cart toward the airport's customs inspection area.

"I've known Gary since 1969," Lila Blake revealed as they walked.

"Only your last name wasn't Blake," Manning said.

"Back then it was Stannard," the woman continued. "My father, Major Stannard, was with the Australian Special Air Service Regiment."

"I served with the Major in Vietnam," Manning said. "We became good friends in the short time we knew each other. Anyway, during a foray into Phuoc Tuy province, her dad took a hit from a Charlie nesting up a tree. I bagged the sniper right after that, but by then the damage was done. Major Stannard died in my arms."

"But before he went he slipped off his wedding ring and gave it to Gary," the woman offered.

"And asked him to hand deliver the ring to you," Katz guessed.

"It was Major Stannard's dying wish," Manning confessed. "And as soon as I could pull some R & R, I hopped a flight into Sydney and brought the wedding ring to Lila."

"And that is how Gary and I happened to meet," the ASIO agent said. If there was more to the story, she was keeping it to herself.

The customs section of the international terminal was a madhouse. It looked as if a week's worth of passengers had descended upon Sydney at once. The area was wall-to-wall people.

"Whoever is handling crowd control," McCarter decided, "ought to get the sack."

"That's not the problem," Lila Blake insisted. "It's the size of the airport. At one time Kingsford Smith, or Mascot, as we Sydneysiders refer to it, was a fair-sized airport. But now, in spite of constant additions, there's just not enough airport to go around."

"So build a new one," James suggested.

"It's been tried," the woman responded, "but unless the powers that be elect to stick it somewhere in the middle of the outback, I doubt that Sydney will have a new airport before the turn of the century. Everyone recognizes the fact that we need it, but nobody wants the noise and congestion associated with an international airport in their neighborhood."

"Meanwhile, the situation here at the existing site continues to get worse," Hahn surmised.

"Precisely," the ASIO agent said.

She directed them toward a set of double doors equipped with an alarm system that she disengaged with a key she took from a pocket in her jacket. She shoved the doors open for the men of Phoenix Force and their baggage to pass through. The doors closed behind her with a metallic click, and she joined the men in a deserted hallway, leaving the human traffic jam of the customs area behind.

"In case there's a pop quiz later, Mr. Wayne," the woman addressed Katz, "let me see if I remember your names." She indicated Karl Hahn. "You're Mr. Frobe."

"I'm Murphy," Calvin James reported.

"And I'm Burton," McCarter said.

Lila Blake grinned at Manning. "What about you?"

The Canadian returned the warmth of her smile with one of his own. "My passport says I'm Mr. Brennan."

"So much for truth in advertising," Lila Blake concluded.

They followed the corridor through a series of twists and turns that eventually opened onto a special parking lot reserved for airport personnel. August was the tail end of Australia's winter, which meant that the morning temperature hovered around fifty-five degrees Fahrenheit. After having spent close to twenty-three hours inside a 747, the brisk air was a welcome change for Phoenix Force.

They followed Lila Blake down a row of parked cars until they came to a Toyota Tórago. Even with the amount of gear they had brought from the States, the luxurious eight-seater had ample room for Phoenix Force and the lovely ASIO contact. Manning rode up front with Lila, while the others made themselves comfortable in the rear of the van.

"We're about ten miles from the city," the woman said as she fired up the engine. "We've booked you into Noah's Northside Gardens in the heart of North Sydney's business district." She backed out of the parking space and headed for the nearest exit.

A MAN SITTING behind the wheel of a blue Calais lifted the microphone of his two-way radio.

"The pigeons have just left Mascot," he reported into the mike. "Be ready with your nets."

Then the man started his car and pulled into line behind the birds he hoped to catch.

9

Lila Blake had no new information to offer on Australia's Nuclear Disarmament Party.

"The NDP's gaining strength every day," she said as they drove into Sydney. "Our records show that the movement is completely on the up and up. Murdering American 'tourists' isn't their style. Getting caught for something like that would throw their political aspirations right out the window."

"Only if they were caught," Manning said.

"True, but at the moment there's nothing to link any known NDP member with the two missing 'tourists' or their slain associate."

Manning nodded. "Agreed. But until we learn otherwise, the NDP and its members top our list of probable suspects." Then because he was curious, he asked, "How much were you told about us, Lila?"

"Not enough to fill a teacup. What I got from this end was simply to expect five special investigators from Washington who were flying down to look around. My job is to offer you ASIO's full support. We were told that the dead American and his missing friends were CIA, so naturally we expected the five of you to be Company men, too.''

''We're not CIA,'' Manning told her.

''Whatever. You have to be highly connected somewhere, though. We don't usually set aside security restrictions so readily. ASIO doesn't make a habit of taking a back seat to foreign operatives working inside Australia. You may not be CIA, but you're not far from it. Special branch of some sort, I would guess.''

The Canadian shrugged. ''Naturally, I'm not at liberty to say.''

The woman across from him laughed. ''Of course not, *Mr.* Brennan.''

While Blake maneuvered the Toyota van through the snarl of traffic that was building as they neared the city, McCarter and James opened several of the suitcases and began passing out weapons. The artillery consisted of guns the men could wear concealed in holsters beneath their coats because they could not go about Sydney openly armed.

McCarter began with a .38 Special Charter Arms snubby revolver that he tucked in a holster at the small of his back. The .38 would serve as a reliable backup piece. The Englishman's primary side arm was the 9 mm Browning Hi-Power that he favored when not depending upon his Ingram SMG.

In addition to the Colt Commander nestled within jackass leather beneath his right arm, Calvin James also carried a G-96 Boot 'n Belt knife inside a sheath attached to the Colt's holster. James's expertise with a knife came with a lot of practice; in Chicago, where he grew up, not all of the butchers in his neighborhood worked behind a meat counter.

Karl Hahn's shoulder rig played welcome host to a Walther P-5 9 mm automatic, while in a similar position Katz wore a SIG-Sauer pistol. The Israeli adjusted the fit of his weapon and then passed Gary Manning's .357 Eagle and holster up front.

As the Canadian slipped off his jacket to put on the holster, Lila Blake questioned loudly enough for everyone to hear, "Not expecting trouble, are you?"

"Not anything we can't handle," Manning replied. "How about you? Are you traveling light or heavy?"

The ASIO agent raised and then lowered her eyes from the rearview mirror. "Today I'm riding with a standard issue Smith and Wesson .38 Police Special," she answered, "but if need be I can use just about anything they make."

"Dangerous lady," James commented openly.

"When I have to be." The woman shifted her eyes back to the rearview mirror. "And who knows? I may just get the chance before much longer."

Manning followed Lila Blake's gaze and swiveled around in his seat. "Something back there we should know about?"

"I'm not sure, but I think we're being followed," she replied. "My intuition says so."

"We've all learned to listen to our instincts," Katz said.

"Right," McCarter added. "It's what keeps our life insurance rates so low."

"Anybody see anything?" Manning asked.

The windows in the Toyota were darkly tinted so there was little likelihood that anyone trailing them would be able to see into the vehicle.

"How about that guy six or so cars back?" James said, pointing. "The pale blue job with the CB antenna on the roof."

Lila Blake checked out the vehicle in her side mirror. "There it is. It's a Calais, I think. I can only see a driver, though."

"He's the only one in the car," Hahn told her.

"And he's yapping to someone on the radio," McCarter observed, reaching into the open suitcase in front of him for his MAC-10. "I may need this after all."

James responded to that possibility by retrieving Katz's Uzi for him. He then handed Hahn a H&K MP-5 machine pistol. Both the Uzi and MP-5 were equipped with noise suppressors.

Lila Blake glanced quickly over her shoulder. "All that extra artillery for one man?"

"Unless he's having a bit of a natter with himself," McCarter said, "he's got friends." The Cockney grinned at Manning and then indicated the open suitcase at his feet. "How're you set, mate? Get 'em while they're hot and all that."

Manning patted the outline of his shoulder holster. "I'll stick with the Eagle for now, thanks."

"I'm fine, too," James decided.

Traffic had momentarily thinned out, and the Calais closed the gap separating the two vehicles by three car lengths. The ASIO woman increased the Torago's speed and pulled away, but the Calais merely accelerated to make up the difference. The impressive skyline of Australia's gateway city loomed directly ahead.

It was easy now for Lila Blake to see the pursuing vehicle in her side mirror. "His technique won't earn high marks," the woman said, "but our shadow is sticking to us like glue. He's still on the radio, isn't he?"

"And chatting up a storm to his pals," Calvin James confirmed.

"Obviously," the ASIO agent stated, "our tail doesn't want to lose us."

McCarter cracked open a window and lit a Players cigarette. "So, don't try to lose him. Is there some place in the city we could lead him that's reasonably quiet at this time of day?"

"Hmmm, there's Hyde Park."

"Ripping choice," the Englishman insisted, "but it's a bit of a drive to London."

"You poms don't hold a patent on the name," Lila Blake said good-naturedly. "We have a Hyde Park of our own. Should we go there?"

"Good idea," McCarter answered, after getting a nod of approval from Katz. "Let's give it a peep. Once we're there, do exactly what I say."

Manning groaned and turned to Lila. "Where precisely do you keep that .38 of yours?"

"Nice guy," McCarter protested.

"I'll be all right, Gary," the Canadian's lady friend told him. "I've been to Hyde Park plenty of times."

Manning jerked his thumb in McCarter's direction. "Yeah, but never on a trip with Mr. Burton."

THE TOYOTA MANEUVERED through the congestion of Sydney's late-morning traffic. Buses, taxis, automobiles and pedestrians all vied for the limited amount of space. The Torago made a series of turns and was soon traveling down Macquarie Street past the State Library, the New South Wales Parliament House and the Sydney Hospital.

The Calais that had followed Phoenix Force from the airport was immediately behind them now. The driver of the four-door sedan was gripping the steering wheel in one hand while holding onto the CB mike that he was speaking into with the other. Hyde Park Barracks and an open-air café were coming up on their left.

"That's Hyde Park in front of us," Lila Blake said.

"Fine," McCarter commented. "Get ready to hit the brakes."

"When?"

"Now!" the Briton ordered.

The ASIO agent did as instructed, mashing her foot to the brake pedal and sending the Toyota into a screeching forward skid. Behind them the Calais was going through similar motions as the car's driver, caught off guard, did everything he could to prevent his vehicle from slamming into the Toyota's rear. Finally, van and sedan came to a halt with little more than the thickness of a postage stamp separating them.

McCarter sprang from the van, turning to his left with his Ingram MAC-10 subgun held in combat readiness. The Englishman's unexpected appearance threw the Calais driver into a panic as he scrambled to throw the car's transmission into reverse.

McCarter poked the business end of the Ingram through the sedan's open passenger window and aimed it directly at the driver's head. "Not today, sunshine. Kill the engine and get out of the car. So much as blink without my approval and they'll be wiping your brains off the upholstery. We understand each other?"

The driver swallowed a lump of fear the size of a cantaloupe. His lips did not move. "Loud and clear, mate."

"You have a gun?"

The driver's eyes shifted nervously to his left. "In the glove box."

"Lucky for you." McCarter stepped back from the sedan. "Scoot out this way, and then we'll go back to my van. Nice and slow. Still with me?"

"Yes."

"Do it like you mean it."

The driver followed McCarter's orders and climbed out of the car. McCarter stepped aside to let the man pass and then followed closely behind his captive as they made their way back to the Torago. Calvin James poked his head out of the eight-seater's sliding door as the pair approached.

"What?" James smiled. "No fireworks?"

"First time for everything," McCarter said.

"Behind you!" James exclaimed, his smile evaporating in a flash of warning.

McCarter whirled in a half circle just as three cars, each coming from a different direction, converged at the Hyde Park intersection. The cars were equipped with all of the extras, including more than a dozen armed men whose assortment of weapons were clearly visible as the vehicles came to a halt.

"Dandy," McCarter mumbled at the unwelcome sight.

A man wielding a shotgun was half hanging out of the window of the car nearest to the Toyota. The ominous barrel of the gunman's Winchester was aimed at McCarter and his prisoner. The driver of the Calais broke into a frantic run toward his apparent rescuers, blocking McCarter's line of fire. The shotgunner fired. McCarter dropped to the street. His fleeing prisoner did likewise as a 00 Buckshot bellyache seared across his middle and sent him writhing to the pavement in a great deal of pain.

McCarter rolled to his right and onto his right knee, his Ingram held tightly in his fist. The shotgunner leaned farther out of his window and corrected his aim. McCarter opened fire before the killer had time to shoot again.

Instantly, the top of the gunman's head disappeared in a spray of red and gray. The body sagged forward, spilling out of the window in a smearing ride to the pavement. Dead fingers spasmed and released the useless Winchester.

The doors of all three attack vehicles opened in unison, and a dozen Nuclear Free Australia zealots rushed out in a stampeding race to see who could claim the first victim. One NFA gunman lifted his SMG to hose down the front of the Torago van. McCarter zeroed in on the killer and hit him with a three-round volley of 115-grain, flat-nosed projectiles. Blood mushroomed across the front of the doomed man's torso as he twitched his way into oblivion.

Phoenix Force hurried to vacate the Toyota before it became their coffin on wheels. Katz, Hahn and Calvin James leaped through the Torago's side door. The Israeli and West German went left to where the Calais sedan was parked. James chose to go to the right toward a waist-high brick wall in front of the open-air café.

Lila Blake managed to grab hold of her .38 S&W just as Gary Manning's powerful fingers grasped her beneath the arms and physically lifted her out of the driver's seat. The Canadian was still pulling the woman toward his side of the van when the driver's side window suddenly ceased to exist.

Manning elbowed his door open and leaned back, letting his weight carry the two of them out of the van. Bullets chattered in a sweep to the right and transformed the windshield into a gaping, jagged hole. Safety glass rained on the Torago's interior. Manning and the woman hit the ground and stayed there while the eight-seater's body was attacked by a swarm of lead. Ugly holes burst from the Toyota's metal skin inches above where the couple lay.

"Where to now?" the woman inquired from within the temporary refuge of Manning's arms.

"I don't know," the Canadian replied. "Fancy a crawl around the park?"

Calvin James dived through the air and behind the brick wall of the café. Subgun fire followed the black warrior's descent. He heard high-velocity whines as bullets connected with stone and mortar. One NFA projectile zipped in and out of the sleeve of his coat, and then James was below the barrier of the wall and scraping to a stop on the not-so-soft sidewalk.

James heard McCarter's MAC-10 erupt once again, followed quickly by enemy shrieks of agony. Then James was rolling out of the way to make room for the Phoenix team's British dynamo as McCarter also sought refuge behind the brick wall.

"How're you doing?" James asked.

"Still in one piece," the Briton reported. "I managed to take out one more of the bastards, which means there's still about ten or so of the yobbos left."

Bullets raked against the wall's opposite side as James remarked, "This is great. We aren't even in the country an hour and already we're under attack before we've had a chance to unpack or take in the sights. What's it take to make friends these days?"

"Another line of work." McCarter replaced the Ingram's spent magazine with a fresh one. "That's better. What do you say we give the beggars back some of their own?"

Katz and Hahn reached the Calais after only a token effort by the NFA strike force to bring the pair down. Other than the occasional bullet directed at the sedan they were using for cover, most of the enemy gunfire seemed to be concentrated on ripping the Toyota van to shreds or hitting Manning and Lila Blake.

Traffic at the intersection leading to Sydney's Hyde Park had ground to a halt as drivers and passengers abandoned their vehicles and fled the scene. But not all of the innocent bystanders caught in the surprise attack were able to safely escape.

Katz and Hahn, unable to prevent the gunman's actions, watched in disgust as a man and woman running for shelter were mowed down by a wild barrage of enemy fire. The killer paused only long enough to confirm that his victims were dead before taking cover behind a Ford Laser.

All but the murderer's shoulder and face were protected when the one-armed Israeli put his Uzi to work, firing a dual three-round burst and blasting his target's head to an instant pile of gray sludge. Two additional NFA fanatics bolted and ran from behind the Ford, showing themselves to an alert Karl Hahn for less than four seconds.

The West German hardcase needed only three. His finger squeezed back on the trigger of his MP-5 and delivered a devastating knockout punch to the NFA duo. Flesh and bone were no match for the deadly H&K. Sprouting miniature red geysers, the gunmen were knocked off their feet and into the gutter where they belonged.

The NFA responded by firing a storm of bullets at Katz and Hahn. One enterprising slug drilled a neat hole through the top and bottom of the Calais's fuel tank. The full tank immediately began to drain and wash over the pavement.

Katz glanced at the steady stream of gasoline that was leaking from the sedan. "I think it's time for us to move on," he said.

"I agree," Hahn replied. "And before things get much hotter."

Gary Manning and Lila Blake watched as Katz and Hahn moved into the open. To the couple's right, James and McCarter were exchanging shots with the enemy from behind the café's brick wall. Several seconds had passed since the last NFA bullet had scored a direct hit on the Toyota van. For the moment, at least, it appeared to the Canadian that he and his Australian friend were in the clear.

"Maybe they forgot we're here?" Lila Blake suggested, also having noticed that the Torago was no longer being used for target practice.

"Maybe they have," Manning agreed, just as he caught sight of three NFA assassins advancing on their position from the opposite side of the van. "Then again, maybe not."

Using a deserted Volvo for cover, the three NFA killers ran toward the Toyota. Only their ankles and feet were visible beneath the parked Torago van as Manning took aim with his .357 and opened fire.

Five times the Desert Eagle roared, each of the semiautomatic pistol's 158-grain bullets connecting as intended. Ankles snapped like matchsticks under the

Magnum's awesome power. Splinters of bone protruded through skin.

All three of the pain-racked gunmen lost their footing and collapsed on the pavement. One of the assassins saw Manning and Lila Blake when he looked beneath the parked Toyota. He tried to tag the pair on the spot.

The two-time loser was still fumbling with his weapon when the Canadian's Eagle screamed once again and switched off the hood's lights forever. Two sharp cracks from Lila Blake's .38 quickly followed, and the recently departed NFA gunman suddenly had company.

"Nice shooting," Manning observed.

"Likewise" was the ASIO agent's response.

"It's too dangerous for us here," Manning said. "Think you can make it to the brick wall?"

The woman nodded. "I'm game if you are."

Manning looked across the thirty feet of open space that separated them from the wall. McCarter and James were still behind the wall, trading shots with the enemy.

Manning waved an arm at McCarter when he saw the Briton huddled in back of the bricks. McCarter returned the gesture. The Canadian tilted his head toward Lila and tapped himself on the chest. He pointed toward the terrorists. McCarter nodded and signaled that he understood. An open palm urged Manning and Lila to stay put.

McCarter said something to James, and then both Englishman and Yank rose to lay down a blazing line of cover fire. The assault took the six remaining NFA hit men by surprise. One gunman never recovered from his shock as Calvin James's Colt stopped him dead in his tracks.

Manning and Lila Blake were on their feet and rushing toward the brick wall the instant McCarter and James went to work. As he ran, Manning sensed movement over his right shoulder; Katz and Hahn were also making for the wall.

The Canadian aimed and fired the final three rounds in his .357 at the NFA cars parked nearby. Lila Blake squeezed off a couple of shots in the same direction. Then she and Manning were ducking behind the brick wall and out of immediate danger.

Katz and Hahn were not as lucky. The Israeli and West German were only fifteen feet from their goal when a pair of enemy subgunners appeared on the scene. Katz's Uzi chattered, and one of the terrorists went down, blood spilling from his bullet-torn body.

The other gunman abruptly tossed his Winchester pump aside and raised his hands in surrender. Katz held his fire and stepped forward. The Israeli wanted to take one of the bastards alive if possible. Dead men do not answer questions about enemy bases.

"Over to the wall," Katz instructed. "Put your hands on the wall and spread your feet."

Suddenly, two additional terrorists made their presence known by pointing their subguns at the Phoenix Force commander. They did not notice Karl Hahn until it was too late. The German commando blasted the pair with a volley of H&K rounds. Parabellum slugs chopped through the chest of one triggerman. The other terrorist caught two 9 mm slugs in the side of the head. His skull popped and brains spurted from twin exit wounds. Both men slumped dead to the ground. Katz had turned sharply when Hahn's MP-5 snarled. The NFA clod who had surrendered took the opportunity to turn the tables on his captors. He moved forward from the wall and grabbed the frame of Katz's Uzi, wrenching it from the one-armed Israeli's grip.

The terrorist stepped back and desperately tried to reverse his hold on the subgun, trying to reach the pistol grip in order to slide his index finger into the trigger guard. Katz did not let him succeed. The Israeli's boot lashed out and slammed between the man's splayed legs. The terrorist groaned in agony as he tried once again to point the Uzi at Katz. The Phoenix Force commander swung his prosthesis. Steel hooks struck the stubby barrel of the Uzi and deflected the weapon away from Katz as the Israeli's left arm rose swiftly and slashed a diagonal karate chop at the fanatic's neck. Katz had planned to hit his opponent in the neck muscle to knock him unconscious, but the hood moved the wrong way at the wrong moment.

The hard edge of Katz's hand struck the terrorist across the throat. The *shuto* stroke crushed his windpipe and demolished the thyroid cartilage. The NFA flunky dropped the Uzi and staggered backward with both his hands clutching his throat. He collapsed to the pavement, drowning in his own blood.

"Are you all right, Mr. Wayne?" Hahn inquired, addressing Katz by his cover name.

"I'm fine," the Israeli assured him. "Get Mr. Murphy over here on the double. We've got to try to save this man. If he dies, he can't tell us anything."

"Murphy?" Hahn frowned, until he realized whom Katz was referring to. "I'll get him."

Police sirens wailed in the distance; the sound echoed through the streets of Sydney. Calvin James ignored it as he joined Katz beside the still body of the last terrorist. The black commando and Phoenix Force unit medic, checked for a pulse and peeled back the man's eyelid. James shook his head.

"You're too good at your job," he told Katz. "Dude's dead. The only way you can question him now is with a Ouija board."

"We might have to answer a few questions of our own," David McCarter remarked as the sirens drew closer. "Well, Ms Blake, I don't suppose you have any pull with the local coppers?"

"As a matter of fact," the ASIO agent answered as she reloaded her revolver, "I do."

10

The odds were a million to one against it happening, and yet the evidence supporting the impossible was staring Sebastian Hardy in the face. His brunch, a festive repast of buckwheat crepes, had been lovingly prepared using only the finest ingredients available. Hardy knew this for a fact because, in addition to being a financial genius, his prowess as a master chef was legendary.

The crepe recipe was flawless. It had *never* failed, yet when Hardy sampled the first bite of the delicacy, he knew that something had gone wrong. His buckwheat crepes tasted like shit.

The reason behind Sebastian Hardy's culinary faux pas was easily isolated. Although lunch was still more than an hour away, the morning had already claimed the lives of more than a dozen members of the Nuclear Free Australia movement.

The last report Hardy had received prior to the dramatic shoot-out at Hyde Park had informed him that a known ASIO agent had met five men who arrived in Sydney on a flight from the United States. The ASIO agent and the five American agents were followed into the city where they were to be intercepted by a NFA reception committee.

The next report Hardy had received had come, not from one of his NFA contacts, but via a special news bulletin broadcast during a cooking class that Hardy was listening to on the radio. According to the bulletin, three carloads of gunmen had clashed with authorities near Hyde Park in downtown Sydney. In the ensuing gun battle two innocent bystanders had been killed as well as all of the unidentified gunmen. There were no other casualties, nor was it revealed what had instigated the shoot-out.

For the first time in his life, Sebastian Hardy had turned off the cooking class in the middle of the program; he was that upset. And that was why he had whipped up a batch of his favorite crepes—the crepes that tasted like shit.

Hardy pushed his plate away in a huff and reached for a toothpick. "Damn!"

"What's the matter, Sebastian?" Lawrence Cheswick asked. In addition to serving as general secretary for the NFA, the smartly dressed Cheswick was also Hardy's right-hand man, a position he had held for twenty years. "Didn't the crepes agree with you?"

Hardy shook an accusing finger at the full plate before him. "What does it look like to you? Have you ever known me to pass up a feast of crepes before? The bloody things just don't taste right."

"This business with the Americans, Seb... I fully expected our people to take care of it with little or no trouble at all. Instead, we're the ones who suffered the heaviest casualties.''

"Obviously, Cheswick, this new bunch of Yanks have a bit more under their hats than the first lot we dealt with. Unbelievable! We have at them with boots and all, and what do we get for our troubles? They take out fifteen NFA guns, and their men walk away without so much as a scratch.

"I don't like the looks of it. Something about these Yanks is very peculiar. I mean, we should have managed to bag at least one of them. The very fact that we didn't leads me to believe they're not your ordinary CIA paper pushers. These boys are something special."

Cheswick dutifully removed the plate of offending buckwheat crepes and deposited them, plate and all, into a nearby garbage can. Cheswick could not recall that Sebastian Hardy had ever lost his appetite before. In twenty years the only meal Hardy had missed was the one he had skipped while on an operating table getting his appendix out.

Once Hardy's desk was cleared and wiped clean, Cheswick asked, "What impact will this morning's confrontation have on our plans?"

"None that I can see. As far as I'm concerned the integrity of Operation Thor has not been compromised. None of the people lost today can be linked to us."

"And the Americans?"

"Yes, well, the Yanks are another story, aren't they? I'm sure that they will go out of their way to find out all they can about the NFA. They're right dangerous, these five Americans.''

"Yes, since none of our people survived their encounter with the Americans," Cheswick felt obliged to point out, "we've lost their trail. They could be anywhere in Sydney.''

"No matter," Hardy announced with renewed confidence. "I know their type. We won't have to look for them. Sooner or later they'll come looking for us. And when they do, *then* we'll know what to do with them.''

"And in the meantime, Sebastian?''

"In the meantime—" Hardy pushed himself away from his desk and pulled himself into an upright position "—if anybody calls, I'll be in the kitchen.''

11

Phoenix Force did not check into Noah's Northside Gardens as originally intended. Colonel Katzenelenbogen's reasons for switching hotels at the last minute was simple. The mysterious attackers outside of Hyde Park obviously knew something about the Force's itinerary. It therefore made sense to deviate from their original plan.

"The evidence strongly suggests the possibility of an ASIO security leak," Katz surmised as he informed the others of his decision. "If so, it's not the first time the security of a nation's special intelligence branch has been breached, and it won't be the last. Offhand, I can't think of any modern intelligence service in the world that hasn't had that sort of problem."

"All well and good," Lila Blake said, verbally coming to the defense of the agency she worked for, "but that doesn't necessarily mean that an infiltrator within ASIO was behind the attack."

"I'm not disputing that," Katz admitted. "But in the absence of proof to the contrary, we have no choice but to react as though the problem does stem from within your department. So, with that thought in mind, is there anywhere else that you recommend we call home during our stay in Sydney?''

Thirty minutes later Phoenix Force had registered under their cover names and had checked into their respective rooms at Sydney's luxurious Regent International Hotel. One of Sydney's ultradeluxe hotels, the Regent afforded the Stony Man crew a spectacular view of the city and harbour.

Spanning the harbour to their left was ''the coathanger,'' officially known as the Harbour Bridge. Below the bridge, the waters of the harbour teemed with seagoing vessels of every description. These included an array of brightly colored sailboats, ships of the Australian Navy, freighters, cruise liners, ferries, tankers, pleasure craft and fishing boats.

Their rooms faced the Sydney Opera House, one of the most recognizable landmarks in all of Australia. Opened in 1972 after more than two decades of planning and building, the geometric shells of the opera house had been constructed on Bennelong Point, a piece of land jutting out into the harbour, and well within the shadows of the bridge.

''Magnificent, isn't it?'' Lila Blake commented as they looked at the opera house.

''Big,'' came McCarter's impression of the structure.

''The opera house is the heart of performing arts in this country,'' the woman explained. ''The building houses four main halls and three restaurants.''

"Yeah, well, maybe next time we pass through town we'll be able to give it a go," McCarter said. "They ever hold any boxing matches there?"

"Not that I know of," the ASIO agent answered. "Now, if you'll excuse me, I should check in with my superiors. They'll want to know what happened earlier."

"And what will you tell them?" Katz inquired frankly.

"The truth. En route from the airport we were subjected to an unprovoked attack and forced to defend ourselves. We survived. Our attackers did not. The aftermath of this morning's gun battle overwhelmingly supports what we already believed."

"Very good," Katz said. "When may we expect to see you again?"

Lila Blake consulted her watch. "How does ninety minutes sound? That should give you gentlemen time to settle in and have a spot of lunch while I issue my report. Plus I'll have to requisition a new set of wheels. The van I picked you up in is ready for the scrap pile."

"Ninety minutes it is then," Katz told her. "Oh, and about our checking into the Regent here, I would appreciate..."

"Say no more, Mr. Wayne," the woman interrupted the Israeli. "If anyone asks where you are, I'll say that, for now, you prefer that your whereabouts remain confidential."

"Will ASIO like that?" Manning wondered.

Lila Blake crossed to the door as the Canadian held it open for her. "No," she admitted. "But that's their problem."

AFTER LUNCH AT KABLE'S, the Regent International's nouvelle cuisine restaurant, Phoenix Force returned to the largest of the two suites they had taken at the hotel. Karl Hahn had performed an electronic sweep of the rooms upon their arrival and had pronounced both suites free of bugs. Assured of their privacy, Phoenix Force openly discussed the details of their current mission.

"I was as surprised as the rest of you when Lila met us at the airport," Gary Manning said to the other members of the Force. "Who would have thought she'd turn out to be our ASIO contact?"

"It's not your fault, Gary," Katz told the Canadian. "You weren't to know. It could have happened to any one of us. We all led fairly colorful lives before we signed on with Stony Man, so it's inevitable that, from time to time, some of the ghosts of our past catch up with us."

"*Some* ghost," McCarter said, whistling. "She's beautiful. A real looker."

"And she carried her own weight in the firefight," James added with sincere respect for the lady's skill. "She behaved like a pro, and that included the way she dealt with the cops. You know the local bluecoats were dying to have a lengthy chat with us, but with Lila there they didn't get so much as a handshake."

"We know we can depend on her if we have to," Manning concluded. "I hate to agree with you in this case, Yakov, but you may be right about security problems within ASIO. Someone sure as hell tipped off our reception committee at the park. Perhaps that tip came from Lila's department."

Katz shrugged. "At this point, who's to know? I imagine it's just as likely that whoever we're up against here in Australia somehow latched onto the roster of all ASIO field agents and had them followed. If so, it could simply be a coincidence that our enemies learned of our arrival so quickly after we landed."

"Exactly," Hahn said. "Our mysterious enemies may have learned about us merely because they already knew about Lila."

The Israeli commando nodded. "And if that is true, then it probably wouldn't have mattered which ASIO agent met us at the airport. The final results, namely the fierce attempt on our lives, would still have taken place."

McCarter sipped from the chilled glass of Coca-Cola Classic that he had brought with him from the restaurant. "What I find dodgy about the whole miserable business is why would the yobs who attacked us risk a strike in broad daylight? Very funny that."

"Unless they thought it was the only chance they would have to bag us all at once?" James suggested.

"I think it's more than that," Manning offered. "If they really wanted to take out the five of us in one go, it would have been easier for them after we checked into the first hotel Lila was supposed to take us to.

"No, my money says our friends tried killing us this morning because our arrival has the potential of disrupting their schedule, interfering with something they've already got in the hopper."

"Yeah," James said, "I can go with that. The five of us could be the *last* thing these people want to deal with now."

"So, who are we talking about?" Katz asked. "The Nuclear Disarmament Party?"

"It's the obvious suspect, Katz," Manning said. "The dead Company man and his two missing colleagues were sent to Australia to investigate the NDP. Something they turned up may have raised a stink."

"So we follow in their footsteps," McCarter decided as he drained his Coke glass dry. "They snooped around the NDP. Let's do the same. Only let's be more open about it, and less under the covers. I'm sure the NDP has offices scattered throughout the country. I'd be very surprised if one of them wasn't right here in Sydney."

"Lila would know for sure," Manning said. "We'll ask her when she gets back."

"If the Nuclear Disarmament Party does have a branch in Sydney, then what?" James quizzed.

"Easy," McCarter replied, a little too casually for Manning's taste. "We pop on over to the NDP for a surprise visit and see what we can dig up."

"When you say 'we,' David," Manning probed, "are you suggesting that all of us pay the NDP this 'surprise visit'?"

McCarter lit a Players cigarette and answered with a smile. "Well, not exactly *all* of us."

12

"How long before we get there?"

"Considering the traffic, another ten to fifteen minutes, I suppose," Lila Blake replied.

"Got that, guys?" Gary Manning spoke as though the rest of Phoenix Force were riding in the same car instead of in a BMW 735i not far behind. "We'll be hitting NDP headquarters in roughly ten minutes or so. Until that time, I'm going off line. I'll start broadcasting again just before we reach our destination. See you then."

Manning felt beneath the buttons of his shirt to disconnect the miniature radio transmitter he had taped to his body.

"There," he said once that was accomplished. "For the next ten minutes we're alone. How've you been, Lila?"

The woman sitting behind the wheel of the stylish ASIO-requisitioned Supra regarded the Canadian with her piercing blue eyes. "I thought you'd never ask."

"Be fair, Lila. You were the last person I expected to see when I got off the plane in Sydney."

"Does that mean you forgot about me, Gary?"

Manning chuckled. "You know better than that. We may have only been together a short while, Lila, but it was quality time all the way."

"Hmmm, it was good, wasn't it?"

"You were one of the few good memories I brought out of the War."

"Next you'll be telling me about the fortune you spent on stamps for all those letters I never received."

"They deliver mail in Canada, too, you know."

Manning's companion laughed. "I'm sorry, Gary. I'm acting like a schoolgirl. Of course, you're right. I could have written you just as easily. I'm not quite sure now why I didn't."

"We were both a lot younger then," Manning said. "We're talking more than fifteen years ago. I suppose neither one of us was ready to settle down. I know I wasn't."

"So, what did you find to occupy your time?"

"A little of this and a little of that."

"And a little of whatever it is you and your four friends behind us get involved in?"

"You got it."

"Judging from the performance you and your friends put on when we were attacked this morning, I'd say you've had a lot of practice dodging bullets and the like."

"Too much practice," Manning confirmed.

"You did say you're not CIA."

"That's right."

"But you're not at liberty to tell me who you really do work for?"

"Right again, Lila. I've told you just about all I can. My friends and I aren't exactly regulars on the evening news, if you know what I mean."

"What I do know is that, even if you aren't CIA, you've got a lot of pull somewhere, or else ASIO wouldn't have agreed to assist you in your investigation. To my knowledge, ASIO has never rolled out the welcome mat like this to *any* other foreign operatives. You obviously have friends in high places."

"The only place to have them, my dear," Manning advised.

"What about a Mrs. Manning?"

"She's now a Mrs. Someone Else. Our marriage didn't exactly set the world on fire, but that's because we were a wet match to begin with. How about you? When did you make the transition from Lila Stannard to Lila Blake?"

"It will be ten years next month."

"Congratulations. What's your husband do?"

"During Vietnam John was with the SAS like Dad. After the War, he was recruited by the ASIO and sent to university on a special education program. That's where we met. John and I were lab partners in a biology class. He and I hit it off straightaway and were married before end of term. We loved each other very much."

"Loved? He's not around anymore, I take it?"

"No. John died in a silly accident three years after we were married. He was in the wrong place at the wrong time. John was working late in a building with a faulty gas main. A leak nobody knew about triggered an explosion. He was killed instantly.''

"I'm sorry, Lila. It must have come as quite a shock.''

"It was, especially so soon after losing Dad.''

"Sure. You still haven't told me how you wound up with ASIO, though.''

"That story will have to wait,'' the woman said. "We're almost at NDP headquarters. Time to go to work.''

"And time for Radio Manning to go back on the air,'' the Canadian said, reconnecting the loose wire to the transmitter he was wearing. "Curtain going up, gang. See you when the show's over.''

NUCLEAR DISARMAMENT PARTY HEADQUARTERS was located on the second floor of a business complex on Sydney's north side. Modestly furnished with a pair of matching beige vinyl settees and a single green plastic chair, the NDP front office reminded Manning of a credit dentist's waiting room. A receptionist in her mid-twenties was there to greet them the moment he and Lila entered.

"Good afternoon,'' the receptionist said. "May I help you?''

"Sure hope so, honey.'' Manning whipped out a handwritten business card and thrust it into the receptionist's face. "Brennan's the name, G. G. Brennan. Good as gold. Perhaps you've heard of me, perhaps not. The important thing...Miss? I don't believe I caught your handle?''

"It's Miss Wilmer."

Manning flashed a smile as genuine as the name on the business card. "Wilmer. Lovely name. Well, *Miss* Wilmer, as you can see from my card I'm with Fanco Productions out of Hollywood. We're about to embark on the most ambitious film in the history of our company, which is why I've stopped by this afternoon. I thought I might have a brief yet meaningful conversation with the NDP's number one man."

Miss Wilmer ran her finger along the page of the agenda book on her desk. "I'm terribly sorry, Mr. Brennan, but it appears that you have neglected to make an appointment to see our director."

Manning burst out laughing and glanced over his shoulder to where Lila Blake had taken a seat on the plastic chair. "Ha! You hear that? *I* didn't make an appointment!" He whirled back to the receptionist. "You're absolutely right, Miss Wilmer, I didn't make an appointment. Don't believe in them."

"Then I'm afraid a meeting with Mr. Roberts is out of the question," Miss Wilmer said with a cool smile. "He does not make a habit of seeing unscheduled visitors."

Manning bent his knees and leaned his elbow on the receptionist's desk. "Tell you the truth, sweetheart, I don't mingle with the rabble fresh off the street either. But do yourself and your boss a favor and take him my card. Tell him that what I have to say won't take anymore than a few minutes of his valuable time, and that we may just be able to come to terms on a deal that will make the whole world respect your Nuclear

Disarmament Party. Will you do that for old G.G., honey?''

Miss Wilmer bit the corner of her lip and then pushed her chair back from her desk and stood. ''Wait here.''

The receptionist disappeared through a doorway to her left. Before Manning could contemplate his next move, the woman returned wearing a surprised expression. ''Please follow me.''

Manning glanced quickly at Lila Blake and then was ushered into the office of Charles L. Roberts, district coordinator for the NDP. Roberts met Manning just as he entered the office and called past the Canadian to Miss Wilmer.

''That will be all for now, Susan,'' he said.

''Shall I bring tea, sir?''

''Not just now, thanks.''

Roberts looked his uninvited guest up and down and then extended his right hand. ''C. L. Roberts.''

''G. G. Brennan.''

They shook hands, and Roberts motioned for Manning to sit directly opposite his oaken desk. Roberts lowered himself into a high-backed leather chair that squeaked when he sat down.

''Miss Wilmer—'' Roberts held up Manning's business card ''—informs me you were most insistent about meeting with me, Mr. Brennan.''

''I never take no for an answer, Mr. Roberts, especially not when businessmen such as ourselves can be so beneficial to one another.''

Roberts tweaked the end of his nose. "You'll excuse me for being so blunt, Mr. Brennan, but I'm a busy man. I have a legitimate appointment scheduled in a quarter of an hour, so if you don't mind, I must insist that you tell me at once exactly why you're here."

"In a nutshell, C.L., the situation is this: Fanco Productions is interested in filming a documentary about the political strength that antinuclear groups are gaining throughout the world. Certainly a thorough examination of the topic would not be complete without including an in-depth study of your Nuclear Disarmament Party."

Charles L. Roberts suddenly lost the bored look that he had adopted when Manning had first entered the office. "A documentary, you say?"

"You got it, C.L. And given that one of your candidates came so close to being elected in the last election, we at Fanco are prepared to guarantee in advance, and in writing, that no less than twenty-five percent of the film will be devoted to NDP activities. But we would need your full cooperation on the project."

Roberts opened an intricately carved humidor and offered Manning a cigar. When Manning declined the smoke, Roberts retrieved one for himself.

"Your proposal's caught me by surprise," Roberts said, lighting his cigar with a wooden match. "It is not surprising that you are coming to us in your hour of need. I am simply amazed that you want to publicize our cause. We have tried for so long to be heard."

"It is not only Fanco Productions that wants to air your message," Manning said. "In fact, Fanco had already been contacted by numerous public broadcasting stations in the United States as well as in Great Britain. They have all expressed interest in airing our documentary as soon as it becomes available. Advance publicity on the project will help to make your Nuclear Disarmament Party famous even before the film is released."

"I can safely say, Mr. Brennan, that the NDP's membership would greet your proposal with excitement."

"I agree. But why has the Nuclear Disarmament Party had trouble informing the rest of the world of its goals?"

Roberts exhaled a puff of smoke. "That's true for the most part, yes. Why do you ask?"

"I was given to understand that you and your members had already been approached by one of our competitors?"

Roberts frowned and shook his head. "Not that I am aware of."

"It would have been three men. Real company types," Manning explained, noting Roberts's reaction to this new direction the conversation was taking. As he watched, Manning saw a line of tension cross the NDP director's forehead.

"We know these three men arrived several days before us," Manning continued, "but since then none of my contacts have seen them. It's almost as if they've vanished into thin air. I'd hate to think that they were on their way back home after successfully cutting a deal with the NDP before I could.''

"You have my word, Mr. Brennan," Roberts insisted. "No one here at NDP headquarters has seen the three men you speak of, nor have I or anyone else associated with the Nuclear Disarmament Party entered into a contractual arrangement with these men.''

Roberts looked at his watch before he nervously announced, "I would love to discuss this matter further, Mr. Brennan, but as I said at the beginning of our conversation, I do have another appointment. Will you be staying in Sydney long?''

"Just long enough to complete my mission, C.L.'' Manning rose from his chair. "Tell you what? Why don't I give you a couple of days to discuss my proposal with your people and then I'll check back with you?''

Roberts got up from his desk. "Excellent idea. And where will you be staying in case I need to get in touch with you?''

Manning upturned his palms. "I haven't really decided yet, C.L. I'd like to look around a bit before I book a room. But when I do find a place to rest my head for the night, you'll be the first to know.''

13

The tail shadowed them all the way back to the Regent International Hotel. Gary Manning was not overly concerned. After the shoot-out at Hyde Park that morning, the Canadian doubted that their opponents would launch another strike so quickly.

The shadow vehicle continued past the hotel, its driver obviously satisfied that Manning and his companion were staying at the Regent. The shadow seemed completely unaware that it had been followed by Katz and his group for the entire length of the ride. Minutes later Phoenix Force and Lila Blake were reunited upstairs.

"How was I coming through?" Manning asked when everyone was assembled.

"Loud and clear," Katz said. "You and C. L. Roberts really hit it off."

"Until I mentioned our missing competitors," Manning said. "If I had kept quiet, we'd probably still be chewing the fat."

"And ironing out the details of Fanco's soon-to-be-released documentary," McCarter said. "Give credit where it's due. It was a good idea."

"I'll say. It's the first one you've had that didn't get me shot at," the Canadian offered.

McCarter looked innocently to where Lila Blake was sitting. "He's always been a kidder."

"What about the two guys tailing us?" Manning asked.

"As far as we could tell they were alone," Hahn said.

"Does that mean we're going to check into another hotel?" James wondered.

"We could," Katz answered, "but in the long run I feel such a move would be counterproductive to our mission. We can't spend all of our time shuttling from hotel to hotel if we expect to accomplish anything of value."

"I don't understand," Lila Blake said. "You checked into the Regent because you thought there might have been a reception committee waiting for you at Noah's Northside Gardens, yet now you're saying it's all right for the enemy to know where you are. Why the sudden change of heart?"

The Israeli smiled. "The odds of our running into a 'reception committee' were considerably greater at that time than they are now. The opposition lost more than a dozen men today. I don't feel they're prepared to hit us at the Regent and risk reducing their numbers by even more."

Lila Blake frowned. "Does that mean you don't expect them to try and kill the five of you again?"

"Not at all," Katz explained. "I would be surprised if they didn't try, but I suspect they will choose the time of their next hit with more care."

"I imagine that it won't be too long from now," James concluded. "My gut feeling says we're not the most popular boys on the block."

"*Ja,*" Hahn agreed. "And we're going to become even less popular with our foes the longer we stay in Australia. The opposition underestimated our capabilities this morning. I don't think they will make that mistake twice."

"Nor do I," Katz said. "Next time they're likely to pull out all of the stops. I believe, as Gary suggested before visiting NDP headquarters, that our continued presence in Australia is most unwelcome. We're becoming an intolerable nuisance."

"That's because we stand to disrupt whatever it is that our friends are planning," Manning added. "Why else attempt to wipe the lot of us out? If they had nothing to hide, they wouldn't have gone out of their way to keep us from looking into their business."

"What could be so important that it's worth sacrificing so many lives for?" James asked.

"Without knowing the face behind the mask of our enemy, that is an impossible question to answer," Hahn supplied.

"My meeting with Roberts went sour once I started playing detective," Manning said. "But that doesn't automatically implicate the whole NDP organization. The fact that Roberts is a key member of the NDP could just be a coincidence. Maybe he's really a bad apple in somebody else's barrel. At this point, all we know for sure is that Roberts liked everything about me except my curiosity.''

"Exactly," Katz said. "And it's that curiosity that's going to get the reaction out of C. L. Roberts and his friends. I'm sure of it.''

14

"I hate bibs," Sebastian Hardy proclaimed. "It's positively indecent that a grown man should have to wear one."

Hardy, nevertheless, lifted the lowest of his three chins and allowed Cheswick to slip the bib into place. Cheswick tied a neat bow behind Hardy's size twenty-two neck before taking his seat at the conference table with the others.

"Much better," Hardy said, smoothing down the bib. "I may hate wearing the bloody things, but I like how they keep my shirts free of spots. There's nothing worse than tucker stains to mar the cut of a tailored garment."

Spread before Hardy was a smorgasbord that would have left many diners green, but not with envy. Traditionally the afternoon was reserved for Hardy's snack time. The gargantuan tycoon had selected an impressive assortment of his succulent favorites to nibble on.

The menu included calf's brains fried in batter, poached beef tongue *à l'alsacienne* prepared with sauerkraut and lean bacon, *animelles*, or sheep testicles, in cream sauce, and grilled pig's ears sprinkled with melted butter and bread crumbs.

Hardy could not fault the snack before him. As he nibbled at a crunchy morsel of calf's brains, he proclaimed, "This emergency meeting of Nuclear Free Australia will now come to order."

Immediately, the ten people joining Hardy at the table stopped eating their pudding and paid attention. One of the first to set down his dessert spoon was Charles L. Roberts, who sat directly opposite Hardy. The NDP member anxiously tweaked the end of his nose in anticipation of being called upon to speak.

"We'll avoid the minutes of our last meeting," Hardy said. "We must concentrate on more urgent matters. All of you, no doubt, are aware of the incident at Hyde Park this morning?"

"Everybody's talking about it, Sebastian," Douglas Rice said. The New Zealander's voice was trembling with worry. "The media has issued conflicting reports on the incident, though. How many NFA members *did* we actually lose?"

Hardy shoveled a forkful of beef tongue and bacon into his mouth as he glanced at Cheswick. "Lawrence?"

"The toll exacted for this morning's unsuccessful venture," Cheswick replied, "stands at fifteen dead. None of the NFA participants involved in the confrontation with our enemies survived the encounter."

"Fifteen," Rice repeated. "And that includes the two Sydneysider pedestrians who were killed? Apparently, if the news reports are to be believed, our people were responsible for gunning them down in cold blood. Is this true?''

Hardy swallowed the beef tongue and speared a stringy clump of sauerkraut with his fork. ''Absolutely not,'' he lied. ''The authorities are obviously attempting to discredit the peace-loving motives behind our cause. Expect such tactics, but do not be alarmed. It is more convenient for the police to blame the deaths of innocents on dead men. No, Douglas, the NFA is not responsible for murdering that poor couple.''

''I'm very relieved to hear that, Sebastian,'' Rice said.

''As are we all,'' Hardy stated, trying to decide which of the tempting delicacies to sample next. ''The purpose of this meeting is to bring everyone up-to-date on the situation. For that reason I've asked Mr. Roberts to join us this afternoon. Mr. Roberts, it would appear, has had the pleasure of speaking face-to-face with one of the men who have come to Australia to destroy us. Perhaps you would share that experience with us, Charles?''

Roberts cleared his throat. ''Yes, well, there's not much to tell. Shortly after lunch today I was visited by a man claiming to be a documentary film producer from America. He gave his name as G. G. Brennan and insisted that my receptionist make allowances for an unscheduled appointment. Naturally, when I was told of this I was instantly on my guard.''

''What made you suspicious?'' Ronald Thompson, the scrawny NFA member, asked.

"Everything," Roberts answered. "Any legitimate filmmaker would have arranged to see me by going through the proper channels, not by storming his way past Miss Wilmer. In any event, I consented to meet with this man to see what his game was. It didn't take me long to wring the truth out of him."

Hardy, who knew Roberts would have difficulty wringing water from a washcloth, much less secrets from a trained CIA operative, prodded the NDP executive for additional information.

"And what did you learn that you can share with us, Charles?" Hardy selected one of the grilled pig's ears and stuffed it into his mouth. "How did you force the man to confess his true plans?"

"It was quite easy," Roberts said. "I encouraged him to ask questions. Once he began, he grew overly confident and gave himself away. He asked me about the three Americans I spoke of last week. Well, now, he may as well have worn a neon sign around his neck after that slipup. This Brennan bloke was no more a filmmaker than anyone here at this table. He was CIA, the same as his mates before him. And he wasn't any smarter than they were, either. After he and his accomplice left NDP headquarters, I had them followed to their hotel. They're staying at the Regent."

"What about his friends?" Sheryl Galloway, the other NFA member from New Zealand, asked. "Witnesses say there were at least four or five men in the other group. Was there any sign of them?"

Roberts shook his head. "No, just the phony film producer and the woman he had driving their car."

Hardy had just opened his mouth to take in a generous portion of the *animelles* when a glob of cream sauce fell from his fork. "See?" he said, pointing to the offending dollop of sauce. "Love that bib! It's saved the day once again." He gnashed the *animelles* to the consistency of paste and swallowed. "The woman this Brennan fellow was with is probably the same ASIO agent who met the group at Mascot this morning. Her name is Lila Blake."

"How did we find out about her, Sebastian?" Ronald Thompson wondered.

"How is it we know about *anything*, Ronald?" Hardy shot back. "It all comes down to buy and sell, my friend, and there's not a whole lot that can't be bought if the price is right. Operation Thor proves that, if nothing else. Thank goodness for greed is what I say—" Hardy devoured another pig's ear before he continued "—or Thor would never have taken flight."

"Now that we know where these CIA operatives are hiding out," another NFA member at the table said, "does that mean we're going to strike the Regent?"

"We could," Hardy confessed. "Certainly, with the number of NFA recruits at our disposal, launching an attack at the Regent would be entirely within our means. We are not going to do so, however."

"Why not?" Sheryl Galloway demanded as strongly as she dared. "If we know that our opponents are staying at the Regent, it would seem foolish not to do everything within our power to eliminate them now, once and for all. And given the limited amount of time before Operation Thor's debut, I don't really see how we can afford to pass up the opportunity.''

"As I said, Sheryl," Hardy explained as he went for the calf's brains again, "we could attack our opponents at the Regent Hotel. That is not the problem. I am simply concerned about the possibility of failure once again. It was no accident that our enemies were able to walk away from this morning's ambush without so much as a scratch while the NFA suffered one hundred percent casualties. It's quite clear that these men are professionals, highly trained to function in complete combat readiness at all times.''

Hardy bit into the beef tongue. "Delicious." He smacked his lips. "As I was saying, sending our NFA recruits against our opponents while they're in familiar surroundings—even if it's just a hotel—would be a mistake. No matter how carefully we might execute such a strike, it's likely that we would be defeated a second time.

"Our recruits aren't fools. Two major losses in one day is hard on morale. It is totally conceivable they would refuse to take up the sword for the NFA cause the next time they're called upon. Our dream, after all, is to live in a nuclear-free Australia, not to die a painful death under a storm of CIA bullets.''

"What do you propose then, Sebastian?" Sheryl Galloway asked. "That we leave our enemies alone? With Operation Thor so near, I don't see how we can risk it."

Hardy contemplated another of the crispy pig's ears. "I'm not suggesting that we abandon the thought of eliminating these troublemakers, Sheryl, but rather that we lure them out of Sydney and deal with them elsewhere. Not only will that enable us to more efficiently dispose of our enemies, but it will also leave the city free from any influence they could exercise over Operation Thor.''

"How *do* we lure these professional killers out of Sydney?'' Thompson questioned.

Hardy devoured the pig's ear. ''We go fishing. If we plan to catch these sharks, we need to use the proper bait. I believe I know what will work. The outcome of their next encounter with the NFA will be different from their first.''

15

Hal Brognola contemplated the ten-inch stack of paperwork before him and wondered for a moment what damage a small bonfire in his office would do? He toyed with the idea as he put a match to yet another cigar, then sighed and started sifting through the pile of paper.

The nation's top Fed had been camped at his desk for the past nine hours, diligently devoting his attention and knowledge to solving one governmental problem after another. He was sure that he had stopped to eat, but he was not sure what it was that he had consumed.

Most of the telexes crossing Hal Brognola's desk were unsettling. The field reports that he was often called upon to analyze rarely referred to incidents that threatened national security. However, the reports painted a grim global picture.

Brognola saw the world as a pressure cooker, a keg of gunpowder floating in a sea of flame. The problem was not deciding *if* a given situation would escalate to the point of requiring Stony Man's expertise but when.

The world's supply of power-mad fanatics was over-stocked.

More than half of the material that Brognola dealt with would never make the six o'clock news; and if it did it would be a highly edited account. The Freedom of Information Act had its place in an open society, but not at the expense of a nation's security. Unless reasonable restrictions and limits were established and adhered to, the act benefited America's enemies and not her friends.

Brognola lifted the next report from the pile of papers on his desk and was almost through the first page when the printer in the far corner of his office began spewing out information. The printer was attached by modem to the same ultrasecure line that linked Stony Man to the White House. It enabled Brognola to continually receive updates from the Oval Office on world events that might be pertinent to the efficiency of the Stony Man teams.

Brognola rose from his chair and made it to the printer just as the transmission ended. He ripped off the printout and carried the report back to his desk. The three short paragraphs left him very concerned.

The Department of Defense had just verified the theft of a single nuclear bomb. It had been part of a shipment en route from the Pantex Ordnance plant outside of Amarillo, Texas, to an undisclosed U.S. Army installation in the Pacific northwest.

The missing nuclear weapon was a "backpack bomb." Weighing only twenty-seven pounds and therefore easily transportable, the bomb delivered a one-kiloton payload. It had the explosive energy equivalent to a thousand tons of TNT.

Although the Department of Defense had launched a full-scale investigation into the matter, it had no leads. Of particular interest was the fact that only one backpack bomb of a set of five had been touched. Updates on the case were promised as they became available.

Hal Brognola felt an icy finger of fear caress his heart. The backpack bomb had been designed so that a single special operations soldier could plant it behind enemy lines. The bomb was light enough for *anyone* to carry, a fact that Brognola found very disturbing.

Too often the world's terror mongers got away with murder...and that was when they were using conventional weapons. What hope could their victims have against the awesome devastation of a nuclear bomb? It could destroy a whole city.

Equally disturbing to Brognola was the revelation that only one bomb had been taken; it was a clear indication that only one was needed.

Needed for *what*, though? Brognola wondered as he shook his head.

16

"That's easy for you to say, mate," Bromly told the dead man. "Too right! You're not the one that has to keep the likes of you company."

Driving up Smith Street past the historic Hotel Vic in Darwin, the capital and seat of government for Australia's Northern Territory, Davy Bromly scratched at the furious itch in his crotch and glanced in disgust at his silent passenger.

"That grunter I picked up last night didn't half know how to do it, but she could have been a bit cleaner, if you catch my meaning," he said. Bromly squirmed in his seat and continued to scratch. "Sure, I should have known better than to dip the wick into such a sorry bit of wax, but a fella's got to have some fun sometime, eh?"

Bromly turned onto Harry Chan Avenue and drove his estate car past the old courthouse and cellblock. The drive through the oldest part of Darwin was always a favorite of Bromly's. The tree-lined streets never failed to relax him when he was on an assignment.

The call from Ronald Thompson had come just as Bromly was sitting down to supper.

"Dig 'em up" were Thompson's terse instructions. "There's been a change in plans."

Bromly looked at the dead man riding shotgun beside him. Some change of plans. The corpse was a right mess, a real pretty sight. Clothes covered with dirt, a ripe smell that brought tears to his eyes and the taste of breakfast to the back of his throat, and finally the small hole in the dead man's skull. His hair was matted with dried blood and bone fragments while the wound itself was packed with sand.

"It's that skinny runt Thompson's fault, mate," Bromly said. "I would have been quite content to leave you and your pal raising the garden."

Bromly's fingers brushed across his swollen lower lip. The swelling was almost gone, and he could just about have a drink without it hurting him all to hell.

Bromly did not know why the third drongo had to go and kick him in the face instead of taking his medicine like the others. But given the unexpected turn of events in Sydney, he guessed things could have been a whole lot worse. He could have lost his life as so many of the NFA members had.

The septic that got away took a bullet with him and lived only long enough to become an outback snack for the dingoes. Good riddance, Bromly thought, running his tongue over his injured lip, although he was still smarting from Thompson's severe reprimand, plus a thirty percent cut in his pay for the job.

Bromly turned another corner and the American's body slumped forward. Bromly blocked the fall by bringing his forearm against the dead man's chest.

"Should have buckled you up," Bromly commented. It was darker outside now. The first of the evening's stars were beginning to shine.

Davy Bromly had not consigned his heart and soul to the NFA or their cause, but he was overly fond of the color of their money. Nuclear Free Australia paid him for what he did best, and he in turn went along with their save-the-world-from-itself mentality.

Bromly held no illusions about his own intelligence, but he knew enough to realize that it would take more than a bunch of freds financed by Sebastian Hardy to go for the big prize that the NFA was shooting for. National defense policy would never be dictated by someone like Hardy despite his obvious wealth and influence. Still, so long as Hardy and Thompson and the NFA needed his talents, Davy Bromly would be on hand to provide them.

The first time that Bromly killed a man was an accident. In need of a little spare change for a night on the town, Bromly solved his cash flow shortage by bashing an old man on the head and stealing his wallet. Bromly had learned two days later that his robbery victim had died before an ambulance could be summoned.

Bromly's second murder was a personal favor to a friend. Ned Clarke had gotten in deep with a local loan shark and come running to Bromly when it was time to pay up.

"I don't have the money," Clarke explained in that whiny voice that Bromly would never forget. "And so they're sending a leg breaker after me. They're gonna kill me, Davy, I swear. What am I gonna do?"

Ned Clarke laid low while Bromly looked into the situation. Bromly soon discovered that his friend was telling it straight. An enforcer for the loan shark was on the scout for Clarke, but before he could locate him Bromly did some serious enforcing of his own. The next morning the dead man's body was discovered floating in Darwin Harbour.

Davy Bromly was now the perfect candidate to become a hired killer. Short one enforcer and convinced that Ned Clarke was somehow responsible for helping his leg breaker to drown, the money hustler let it be known that Ned Clarke's head was worth a thousand dollars.

"What am I going to do now?" Clarke moaned as he threw his few belongings together in a bag. "I'm really up a gum tree this time, Davy. The bastard's put a price on my head. One thousand dollars!"

"Don't worry about it," Bromly told Clarke. "I took care of everything."

"You did what? You mean you sent him for a final swim, too?"

"No, but I did the next best thing."

"What's that, Davy?" Ned Clarke asked. "What's the next best thing?"

"I told him that I'd take his thousand dollars."

And Bromly promptly pulled the trigger of his gun to earn the loan shark's gratitude. Friends were friends, but business was business. To Bromly's way of thinking, no one's life was worth more than keeping his bank account well fed and healthy. It was a philosophy that he had decided to follow earnestly.

Satisfied that it was now dark enough for him to go to work, Bromly left Darwin's picturesque historical section and drove across town. There was room in the back seat for three, but if someone rode on the floor he could squeeze in four.

Bromly rounded a corner and spotted an old man with a limp walking a small dog. He sped down the block, pulled to the curb and got out. There were no other pedestrians on the street and traffic was sparse in both directions.

Bromly hid and waited behind a tree. When the sound of approaching footsteps grew closer, he walked out into the open.

"Hang on," Bromly said.

"Wha...?" The old man stammered. "Who, who are you?"

"I caught your limp, friend, so I thought I'd offer you and your mutt a ride in my car."

"We can walk, thanks."

"I'm not asking you, mister. I'm telling you. Come for a ride in my car. I ain't got all night."

The old man shook his head and tried to back away. "Don't...don't hurt me," he pleaded.

"Now, why would I do that?"

Before his victim could react, Bromly grabbed the old man by the front of his shirt and plunged a knife into his chest with the other hand. The elderly gentleman inhaled sharply and opened his fingers, releasing the dog's leash. The frightened animal went running, whimpering with high-pitched yelps and dragging the leash behind. Bromly watched the dog run away, then removed the blade and stabbed the man again.

"No..." Bromly's victim weakly protested before his body sagged to the ground. Bromly took special care to hold it away from him so that he would not get any blood on his clothes. He hefted his prize to the back seat of his car and dumped it inside, then climbed behind the wheel.

"What do you say, fellas?" he called as he drove. "One down, three more to go. Who said it's hard to throw a good party? Not us! We're living proof they're wrong."

Bromly's next unwilling passenger was a woman in her mid-thirties. The woman died after Bromly played hide-and-seek with the blade of his knife. She was dead before she could scream.

Back on the road once again, Bromly decided to drive to another part of town. He only needed a couple more bodies and then he was in business. Thompson's instructions from Sebastian Hardy had been very specific, and Bromly intended to follow them to the letter. He had already made one error that week.

"Just two bodies away from the end of the ride," Bromly told the dead man to his left. "Then it's everyone out for a stretch so we can set the stage for some real fun. You'd like that, right? 'Course, you would. Me, too. We'll have some fun and maybe you'll quit looking like you've just lost your last friend. It wasn't my idea to send your partner packing, but fair is fair. I never told you before, but he wasn't exactly the life of the party.''

The killer scratched at the itch terrorizing his groin. ''Never take a grunter to bed, mate. It just ain't worth it.''

ARTHUR FRENCH CARRIED THE BODY ashore and walked to the closest beachfront cabana. The lights were on, and through the glass doors French could see three people. A man and two women. They were laughing and drinking, obviously enjoying their conversation. They were precisely the guests French required.

Carrying his grisly companion as close to the cabana as he dared, French lowered the body to the ground and then went the rest of the way on his own. He needed to be swift and he was. He tested the cabana's side door and found it unlocked. He quickly tugged the door open and marched inside.

''What's this?'' one of the women asked in surprise when she saw him enter. ''Who are you?''

Before the woman or her friends knew what was happening, French produced his noise-suppressed handgun and opened fire. The lady with the questions went first, one bullet drilled neatly through the forehead and the next through her left cheek. The impact of the twin blasts lifted her from her feet and threw her back onto the double bed.

Unable to move, the remaining man and woman were disposed of as quickly as French could work the trigger of his gun. He left the bodies where they dropped, then quietly went back outside to retrieve the cabana's newest resident.

17

"Nothing like a ray of sunshine to brighten the end of the day," McCarter decided as the evening news on Channel Ten concluded. "Comforting, isn't it, to know that we northerners haven't cornered the market on madness?"

The news program had led off with a report on two unrelated incidents of multiple homicide. The first case concerned five unidentified victims found in Darwin's Botanical Gardens. All but one of the deceased had been stabbed to death.

The second incident occurred at The Resort, a holiday hideaway on Dunk Island, off the northeast coast of Australia and not far from the Great Barrier Reef. Four bodies had been discovered in one of The Resort's cabanas. Each of the four, two men and two women, had been shot in the head.

The bodies had just been discovered, and therefore the amount of information available was minimal. Viewers were advised to stay tuned for additional updates.

The closing news story concerned a trade conference to be attended by the Commonwealth nations. It was scheduled to get underway the following day in Sydney. After that the program's credits began to roll. James crossed to the television and turned the set off. "Ray of sunshine, my ass," he said, looking to McCarter. "What's wrong with the world that things like mass murders happen?"

The members of Phoenix Force had returned to the largest of their two rooms to discuss their next move after having a late dinner. Although he still believed that Manning's meeting with the NDP man, C. L. Roberts, would prompt their enemies to attempt another strike against them, Katz was the first to admit that the response he expected was long overdue.

"Maybe we hurt them more than we thought this morning?" Manning suggested. "Losing fifteen men would be devastating if they only had twenty or so to begin with."

"Somehow I don't think that explains our opponents' inactivity," Hahn countered. "I feel our foes are holding back, not for lack of additional personnel to throw at us, but because they want to make absolutely sure that when they finally do move against us there isn't the slightest possibility of failure."

"I must agree with Karl," the Israeli unit commander of Phoenix Force said. "Our friends are waiting for a sure thing. We know they are aware that we're registered here at the Regent, yet each passing hour makes it increasingly clear that they don't consider this hotel an acceptable battleground. They want to choose the site of our next confrontation. And as long as we remain at the Regent, we deny them that choice.''

The telephone rang, and Manning answered it. He listened for a few seconds, said something to the caller that the others were unable to hear and then brought the conversation to a close.

''That was Lila phoning from the lobby,'' the Canadian explained when he replaced the receiver. ''She's on her way up and wanted to let us know so that we'd be expecting her.''

''Did she say anything else?'' Calvin James inquired.

''Yeah,'' Manning replied. ''She said there's been a breakthrough of some kind.''

''Crikey!'' McCarter announced with a half-smoked Players dangling from the corner of his mouth. ''It's about bleedin' time.''

Two minutes later Lila Blake arrived. ''We've had a breakthrough,'' she said almost immediately.

''So Gary tells us,'' Katz offered. ''At this point we could use one. What's happened?''

''Were you watching the news tonight?'' she asked.

''On Channel Ten,'' Manning confirmed. ''The feature stories were about some murders up in Darwin and in a place called Dunk Island. Did we miss something on another channel?''

''No, that's the one,'' she replied.

''I don't get it,'' James said. ''How does the fact that nine people were killed tonight tie in with us?''

"Simple," Lila Blake told him. "For starters, two of the victims were already dead before the others were murdered."

"Hmmm," Hahn mused aloud. "And have the two been identified?"

The ASIO woman nodded. "They have. They're the two missing partners of the dead CIA agent we've already identified."

"Bloody hell!" McCarter practically spit out his cigarette. "How long had they been dead?"

"We don't know for certain," she said, "but judging from the condition of the bodies several days at least. Evidently both bodies had been buried and exhumed. The one found in Darwin had both its legs broken, but apparently that damage was inflicted long after the victim was dead. Most likely to allow the body to be easily transported."

James shivered. "That's creepy. Kill a guy, bury him, dig him up and then break the dude's legs so he can go for a ride. We're dealing with a real tasty bunch."

"Lila, what about the other missing agent?" Katz asked. "I take it his body was discovered elsewhere? Dunk Island, perhaps."

"Bingo," she stated. "He was found stretched out on a bed in one of The Resort's cabanas as if he were taking a nap. Except for the gunshot wound to the back of his head, his body was unharmed. Both of the slain CIA agents, incidently, were killed the same way, and apparently with the same weapon. Ballistics should have a definite on that by morning."

"Does ASIO have any clues as to how the other victims fit in?" Manning wondered.

"So far, we're reading it as window dressing," the Canadian's friend responded. "Also, given the distance between Darwin and Dunk Island, along with the murder weapons involved, and the approximate time of death of the remaining seven victims, it's likely that we're dealing with at least two killers. The timing of the killings makes it impossible for them to have been committed by the same individual, although they are definitely related."

"Wonderful," Manning commented dryly. "The more the merrier."

"I don't suppose," Katz said, "that anyone is claiming responsibility for the murders?"

Lila Blake surprised them all by answering in the affirmative. "That's the other news I have. They're calling themselves the NFA."

"The *NFA*," James repeated. "What's it stand for?"

"Nuclear Free Australia," the woman answered.

"How much does ASIO have on them?" McCarter asked.

"Not a thing," came the reply. "Until this evening we didn't even know that the group existed."

"How did this NFA take credit for the crime?" Katz asked.

"In each case," the woman said, "letters were folded and left in envelopes on the chests of the slain CIA operatives. Both letters were run off on the same dot matrix computer printer, but that's as much as we have right now."

"Tracing the letters back to the printer would be impossible," Hahn admitted. "It would require doing comparison printout checks with every computer owner in the country."

"ASIO is hoping that something else they can use will turn up," Lila Blake informed them. "Time is definitely on the NFA's side, though. This information wasn't released to the media, but the letters claiming responsibility for the murders also promised that more people would be killed in Darwin and on Dunk Island by this time tomorrow night."

"Unless *what*?" James wanted to know. "What outrageous demands did this NFA outfit make to insure that no more innocents are killed?"

"There were no demands," the woman said. "The letters identified the NFA and promised more deaths and that was it."

"How about fingerprints?" a hopeful Manning asked.

"None," the ASIO agent replied. "Each of the letters was spotlessly clean."

McCarter finished his cigarette and quickly lit another. "A bit dodgy, isn't it? This NFA, I mean. Usually these types justify their actions by claiming to right some wrong by making demands, yet here we have a group that's doing just the opposite."

"Maybe they're waiting to stage something more spectacular before they make their demands," James surmised.

"In either case they're probably not going to appreciate the fact that no mention of the Nuclear Free Australia movement was leaked to the press," Lila Blake concluded. "It was an ASIO decision to withhold any reference to the group, at least until we can learn more about them."

"It's a move I can respect," Manning said. "If extremist groups weren't pampered like glorified movie stars whenever they pull one of their terrorist stunts, most of them would soon crawl back under the rock they came from. Kick the scum off the publicity gravy train that they usually ride on and most of the killers would never get their act together in the first place."

"But back to Lila's point about the NFA not getting coverage on the news," Hahn said. "If they did kill all those people simply for attention, then it's reasonable to assume that not getting that publicity will rouse their anger. On the other hand, perhaps it does not matter to them whether or not the public knows who they are. It might be enough to suit their present motives that only *we* know about them."

"That's the theory I support," Katz said. "I think this miserable display tonight is just the NFA's way of letting us know where they are."

"I wish we had more on their background," Lila Blake said.

"We actually know more about the NFA than is readily apparent," Hahn indicated. "Since it appears that the missing CIA operatives were killed by the NFA while the American agents were investigating

Australia's Nuclear Disarmament Party, while by no means implicating the NDP in the agents' deaths, it does establish a possible link between the two groups.''

The Aussie woman shrugged. "And yet ASIO has never found the Nuclear Disarmament Party suspect or guilty of any questionable practices.''

"That could mean any number of things," Mc-Carter said. "The NDP could be totally innocent. Or if they are involved with the NFA, it could mean that the group excels at covering its tracks. Finally, a third option suggests that Nuclear Free Australia could be a splinter group made up of present or former NDP members with the bulk of the Nuclear Disarmament Party completely unaware that the NFA even exists.''

"That's not the impression I got from C. L. Roberts," Manning said. "Roberts knows something. I'm sure of it."

"I could easily have ASIO pick him up for questioning," Lila Blake offered.

"That would be fine if we knew for sure that Roberts is in deep with the NFA," Katz said. "Since we don't, picking him up now could do more harm than good by alerting the rest of Nuclear Free Australia that we know more about their activities than they think. For that reason, I say leave Roberts be for now. But I would like your people to put Roberts under twenty-four-hour surveillance so that his actions can be monitored around the clock.''

"No problem, Mr. Wayne," Lila Blake answered, using Katz's cover name. "I'll have ASIO shadow Roberts for as long as you like. We can double-team him, which will give us an extra blanket of security should Roberts somehow give his first shadow the slip."

"Excellent," Katz decided.

"No one has brought it up," Calvin James said, "but there's the financial aspects of the NFA to consider as well. Murder and mayhem don't come cheap. Somebody has to be footing the bill for their game.

"If monetary funding is coming from abroad, we'll be hard pressed to uncover the source without a lot of legwork and luck. However, if the money enabling the NFA to operate originates here in Australia, that puts a different light on the subject." James turned to Lila Blake. "How difficult would it be for ASIO to come up with a list of all Nuclear Disarmament Party members? Current and past membership would be best, with as much financial background on them as you can obtain."

Lila Blake smiled. "I'm sure the NDP has a list that they wouldn't mind loaning us. ASIO could probably produce such a list in under an hour. The financial information on NDP members will take longer, but I can have my people work on it through the night."

"That should narrow our prospects considerably," James told her, then he signaled to Katz. "That brings us back to Darwin and Dunk Island. You're convinced it's the NFA's way of issuing a challenge to us?"

"And of getting the five of us out of Sydney," Katz added. "This lets them choose the time and place of our next confrontation."

McCarter impatiently ground out his smoke in an ashtray. "As well as effectively splitting us up. We can't all be in both places at once. Who's going where?"

"You and Gary can check out Darwin," Katz informed the Briton. "The rest of the Force will head for Dunk Island."

"Hold on." Lila Blake's protest was immediate. "What happened to teamwork? You're all in my homeland, remember? So where's that leave me while you're hopping about the country?"

McCarter opened his mouth to speak, but an alert Manning cut the Cockney off. "You can come to Darwin with us. We'd love to have you." Manning looked at McCarter for confirmation. "Wouldn't we, Mr. Burton?"

"Loverly," McCarter mumbled.

"It's settled then," Katz said. "What about transportation? Any recommendations, Lila?"

"If you don't mind booking a commercial flight," she answered, "we can catch Ansett out of Kingsford Smith in the morning. That will get us out of Sydney before 8:00 A.M."

"That will be fine," Katz assured her.

"What about after we reach our destinations?" the ASIO woman asked. "How do you gentlemen plan to find this Nuclear Free Australia group?"

Katz returned grimly, "Somehow, I think the NFA will give us all the help that we need."

18

"It's a morning like this that gives a man an appetite," Sebastian Hardy said, sinking his fork into a shrimp and Swiss cheese omelet covered with Tabasco sauce. Hardy opened his mouth, and a quarter of the omelet disappeared in a single gulp. Sauce dribbled down his chins, but the Australian financier ignored the mess and continued eating.

The remaining people at the table, the governing core of the Nuclear Free Australia movement, were also enjoying breakfast. Sebastian Hardy was not one to play favorites, which was why everyone else had been served a bowl of cereal, a slice of buttered toast, one strip of bacon and a glass of orange juice made from frozen concentrate.

Another quarter of his omelet vanished as Hardy washed it down with a gulp of freshly squeezed lemonade. His thirst quenched for the moment, he returned the glass to the table and proceeded to tap against it with the end of a teaspoon. The tinkling sound of metal on glass soon quieted everyone to Hardy's satisfaction.

"Good morning one and all," Hardy officially greeted his fellow NFA members. "You're probably wondering why I asked you here today?" He laughed out loud, and those present dutifully followed his example with polite laughter of their own. "Seriously, dear friends, you all know why you're here. After an incubation period of nearly eighteen months, a substantial outlay of cash and, most recently, the tragic loss of fifteen of our colleagues, the day we've all worked so hard for has at long last arrived." He raised his glass of lemonade. "A toast, dear friends, to Nuclear Free Australia's mission. A toast to Operation Thor!"

Nine glasses of orange juice were raised in unison as the members repeated Hardy's toast in a chorus of strength.

"To Operation Thor!" they proclaimed.

Each person drained his or her glass in unified recognition of the NFA's mandate. Hardy was the first to finish; Sheryl Galloway was the last.

"That's better," Hardy said, smacking his lips. "I know we still have numerous little details to tend to today, but I think it's safe to say that by this time tomorrow the whole of the modern world will be praising the NFA.

"Because of our beautiful vision, and our commitment to the preservation of future generations, the people of our planet will be shown that there is an alternative and that nuclear weapons threaten us all. The global community has no need of these weapons. The uranium deposits of this vast land should be used only to generate nuclear power. We, the governing board of Nuclear Free Australia, know it. After the success of Operation Thor, the rest of the world will know it as well.''

Hardy paused for the applause he expected and was not disappointed. When the clapping died, Hardy again rapped on his glass with the teaspoon.

''Thank you. Thank you,'' he said, forking another fluffy mouthful of omelet down the hatch, consigning the food to the gastric whims of his overworked digestive system. ''As fate would have it, our reason for celebrating today is twofold. I believe, Mr. Thompson, you could elaborate on the matter?''

The ultrathin Thompson looked up from his bowl of cereal. ''Indeed, I can, Sebastian.'' He raised his napkin to wipe his lips and then pulled himself out of his perpetual slouch. ''It's no secret that we've been watching the five men staying at the Regent. It was due to their intervention that Nuclear Free Australia suffered its first major setback in the history of our organization.

''Just prior to sitting down with you for breakfast, I received telephone confirmation of the news we've all anticipated, namely that our five enemies have checked out of their rooms and are now on their way north.''

''Do we know for certain which city they went to?'' Douglas Rice asked.

''We do,'' Thompson answered. ''The five, as well as the ASIO agent who has been assisting them since their arrival, were followed by two of our people to

Kingsford Smith. There, separate bookings were made on Ansett to Darwin and Cairns. Cairns is the closest airport to Dunk Island.''

"Splendid!" Hardy exclaimed. "By dividing their ranks our enemies have made themselves more vulnerable to our NFA reception committees once they reach their destinations. Were our people able to determine which of the five went where?''

"Yes," Thompson said, and then went on to supply that information to Hardy.

"What about the woman?" Galloway inquired.

"She boarded the plane with the pair going to Darwin," Thompson replied. "Both flights departed around eight this morning."

Hardy stabbed at the last of his Tabasco-dripping omelet as he commented, "That will provide us with ample time to put Bromly and French on alert."

"How many NFA members will they have at their disposal?" Cheswick asked.

Thompson was quick to answer. "Bromly has access to at least twenty guns. That is, of course, if he uses his full allotment."

"Which he damned well better," Hardy warned. "I don't want a repeat of yesterday's fiasco. You tell that gumsucker Bromly that I'll hold him personally responsible if these people escape. We're handing him our enemies on a bloody silver platter, so there will be no excuses. You tell him I said to use every available NFA regular that he can get his hands on. After yesterday, he'd be crazy not to."

"Ahem, yes," Thompson said, coughing. He ran a nervous finger around the inside of his collar as he thought to himself that Bromly wasn't the only lunatic in the bunch. "I'll relay your orders exactly as you've told them to me."

"Good." Hardy fed the final bite of omelet into his mouth and asked as he chewed, "What about Arthur French? How's he set on Dunk Island?"

"French and his men will outnumber our opponents roughly six-to-one," Thompson said. "Not much of a contest taking into account that one of the three American agents French will be facing is a one-armed septic who's only a short step this side of a pension."

"Even so," Hardy cautioned, "French should be careful. I seriously doubt the 'old man' lost his arm biting his fingernails. The fact that he wears a prosthesis didn't seem to hamper his performance yesterday. He's more than your average nine-to-five paper pusher. He's a combat veteran and so are his friends. Give French the same message Bromly gets."

"Right," Thompson promised.

"The knowledge that our opponents are unwittingly flying to their own funerals carries with it a sense of inner peace," Rice confessed. "I only wish that we could be with Bromly and French to witness the well-deserved demise of these American meddlers.

"The United States cannot be allowed to callously pollute the high seas with a floating arsenal capable of triggering World War III. The Americans haven't given one thought to the people caught in the middle. And now the Washington warmongers have seen fit to export a team of trained killers to our shores to promote a foreign policy that was doomed to failure from the beginning. I say that whatever Bromly and French do with the bunch is too good for them, and a far sight better than the likes of them deserve.''

''Knowing Davy Bromly and Arthur French as we do,'' Thompson pointed out, ''I'm sure we won't be disappointed with how they handle the Americans. If they can so brutally liquidate members of the general public, can what they have in store for the Americans be any less fierce? I think not.''

Sebastian Hardy looked about for something else to eat and settled upon the slice of bacon remaining on Cheswick's plate. ''For our purposes all that's really important is that the bastards' Aussie holiday come to an abrupt end in Darwin and Dunk Island. How Bromly and French care to go about that is their business. Frankly, if it gets the job done, I don't mind if they bloody well execute the Americans on the evening news.

''Nuclear Free Australia holds the future of the human race in its hands and I, for one, am not prepared to abandon our righteous cause when we are finally so close to achieving our goal. I harbour no doubts that Bromly and French will kill the Americans and be done with it. We won't be troubled by them again.''

Hardy's stomach grumbled, prompting more than one NFA member at the table to wonder if they had just heard a roll of thunder. Hardy patted his belly and barely concealed his frown when he saw that Cheswick's cereal bowl was empty. In mild desperation he fumbled in the pockets of his suit coat until he was rewarded with the discovery of a lone caramel toffee that he had previously overlooked. Hardy twirled the cellophane wrapper off the piece of candy and popped the toffee into his mouth, tucking it in the side of his cheek.

"With the exception of Thompson and Cheswick," a contented Hardy continued, "the rest of you are not fully aware of how we were able to lure the Americans out of Sydney."

"To catch sharks you need the right bait," Sheryl Galloway pronounced. "Isn't that what you said, Sebastian?"

"It's the only way to land the big ones," Hardy confessed.

"So how did we land *our* big ones?" Trevor Jenkins asked. He was a senior NFA leader from Perth on Australia's west coast. "What bait did you use?"

"I gave the Americans back something they lost," Hardy said as he smiled, estimating that he still had a good three minutes worth of toffee if he took it real slow. "I gave the Americans back their missing CIA agents."

"What?" Trevor Jenkins leaned forward in surprise. "But you told us Davy Bromly buried the two men after he killed them?"

"Bromly did," Hardy confirmed, "but I had him dig the pair up again. I figured it was the fastest way to get a reaction out of our friends, and I was right. I had one of the bodies turn up in Darwin and had the other sleeper shipped to Arthur French so he could deliver it fresh to Dunk Island.''

''But why would all of the Americans and their ASIO contact leave Sydney?'' Rice questioned. ''Couldn't they have had the bodies flown south?''

''Not really,'' Hardy corrected, noting that he had two more minutes on his toffee. ''You see, an envelope containing a letter was left with each dead man. The letters promised that more residents of Darwin and guests of Dunk Island would be murdered today, which is why Bromly and French did away with the seven people last night. We wanted the authorities to take our threat seriously.''

''I don't understand,'' Sheryl Galloway said, pushing her half-eaten bowl of cereal to one side. ''I watched the news report yesterday evening and read about the murders in this morning's *Herald*, but I don't remember any mention of the two slain CIA agents or any of the death threats in the letters.''

Hardy was feeling positively cheerful with a minute to go on his toffee. ''Of course not. The authorities didn't release the information about the two dead CIA men because of the disgusting hand-holding that goes on between our two governments. And the death threats weren't made public because the wallopers obviously want to avoid a panic. Unless I'm mistaken, The Resort at Dunk Island has 140 rooms. A panic there would transform the place into a deserted island. Bad publicity all the way around.''

"Hmmmph," Jenkins complained. "Who can trust the reliability of today's news when they omit such pertinent information and can't get a simple story straight?"

Thirty seconds until the toffee dissolved. "That's not the half of it, Trevor."

"There's more?"

"Yes," Hardy said. "Both letters were signed by the NFA!"

Hardy had expected this latest disclosure to shock most of those sharing his breakfast table. He was not disappointed. Jenkins choked on his cornflakes. Rice went through the same motions with a mouthful of orange juice. Sheryl Galloway reacted by biting her lower lip.

"Sebastian!" Jenkins was the first to speak. "You can't be serious? You actually signed Nuclear Free Australia to the letters left with the bodies?"

"At the bottom of each of them," Hardy confirmed. His toffee was on its final five-second countdown, and already his eyes were scanning the table for what food remained. "Can you think of a better way to lure our enemies out of Sydney?"

Jenkins shrugged. "Not off the top of my head I can't, but that's not my point. Given some time I think we could have come up with an alternative plan."

"I happen to disagree," Hardy said. His toffee was history now, and he was beginning to feel irritable. "With Operation Thor virtually upon us, there was no time to indulge in group planning sessions. I saw what had to be done and acted accordingly."

"I think Trevor's real concern," Sheryl Galloway noted, "is that by linking us with the murders up north our future credibility may have been irrevocably damaged."

"Rubbish." Hardy dismissed the New Zealander's notion with a wave of his pudgy right hand. "Once the world has comprehended the full impact of Operation Thor, they'll forget the affair up north."

Hardy casually grabbed a half slice of toast from Cheswick's hand and began to eat it. "What all of us must remember as we prepare to embark upon our finest hour is that, come tomorrow, Nuclear Free Australia will be known internationally. We are prophets of a new age who took the bold steps necessary to lead the human race out of darkness. What we must never forget is that Operation Thor heralds the beginning of the total nuclear disarmament of every nation on earth. Generations to come will revere us all as heroes."

"I didn't mean to imply otherwise," Jenkins insisted.

Hardy gobbled the last bite of toast and licked his buttery fingers clean. "I know that, Trevor, because if I felt that you *had* lost faith I would personally buy you a front row seat for this evening's performance." He nodded to Cheswick. "Besides breakfast, Lawrence, what else do we have on our menu for today?"

Still hungry, and wishing that he had eaten his meal a little faster, Hardy's right-hand man consulted the day's upcoming agenda in a spiral-ringed pad that he always carried with him. "You have a luncheon at noon with the chairman of the Sydney Orphans' Benevolent Society. I understand they'll be serving *Carré d'agneau aux nouilles*."

Hardy's brown eyes lit up. Loin of lamb with noodles was one of his favorite meals. "I can almost taste it. What about this afternoon?"

"At 2:30 you're meeting with the president of Hungerson's, the new restaurant chain you were thinking of investing in. My spies tell me he's out to win your support with a *Zampino* recipe that's been in his family for years. He'll be complementing the dish with a delicate potato puree."

"Bless his heart," Hardy said, pleased with his extraordinary good fortune. *Zampino*, or stuffed pig's leg, was another of his favorite meals. "And after my meeting with this Hungerson man we will hold our final get-together here."

Cheswick nodded. "That will be at six o'clock, right after your first supper, at which time we will officially hold the drawing to determine who the lucky Nuclear Free Australia member will be to win the privilege of raising the curtain on Operation Thor.

"The helicopters arrive at your estate promptly at 7:30 to take us to the airport, and by 8:30 we will all be in the air and bound for Auckland. One hour later Operation Thor will usher in the dawn of humanity's nuclear-free lease on life." Cheswick closed his notebook. "I believe that covers the day, Sebastian."

"Then we may as well adjourn," Hardy said. "But before we do I think it only fair that everyone be given a closer look at the individual responsible for making our dreams a reality. It is with great pride that I introduce to you the morning's guest of honor, the star of Operation Thor.''

Hardy pressed an ivory-colored button in a small control console in the arm of his chair. Immediately, two oak panels in the center of the dining table silently drew apart. A motor switched on, and then the ''star'' rose majestically into view.

Sheryl Galloway's voice cracked with emotion. ''I had no idea it would be like this.''

Cheswick's eyes grew misty. ''A work of art.''

Douglas Rice and Trevor Jenkins added simultaneously, ''A masterpiece!''

''I confess I thought it would be larger,'' Cheswick said. ''It's really quite small.''

''But it's big enough to get the job done,'' Hardy announced proudly.

''How much *does* it weigh, Sebastian?'' Jenkins asked.

''Twenty-seven pounds,'' Hardy answered.

Only Thompson remained quiet. He sensed that the ''guest of honor'' would doom them all.

19

The man with the bomb did not expect to get caught. He had better things to do with his time than spend it behind bars. Besides, who would suspect a camera-toting tourist of doing such a thing in the first place?

The man rode the bus as far as the Circular Quay and then got off. Going through the motions of a typical tourist, he stopped at a souvenir shop and purchased postcards and several rolls of film. Farther up the street, at a newsstand, he bought a Gregory's pocket map of Sydney. Each of the items he acquired was deposited inside the camera case that was draped carefully over his left shoulder.

The man crossed the street to the corner of Pitt and Alfred and passed by the Ship Inn Hotel. He slowly made his way through the sea of tourists jostling for space on the sidewalk. The man was not overly fond of people, especially not when they seemed to be deliberately going out of their way to keep him from reaching the Sydney Opera House.

The man had been a member of Nuclear Free Australia for less than a year. During that time he had never been called upon to do anything more dangerous than write anonymous letters of complaint to politicians whose blind devotion to an insane nuclear-based defense strategy had brought Australia to the brink of total annihilation. All of his letters had been ignored, and now his beloved homeland was closer than ever to the complete destruction that would consume the island continent unless drastic measures were taken.

The bomb that he carried would take care of that. Under normal circumstances he would have been opposed to hurting anyone, but the decision was no longer his. The majority of Australia's population might be willing to silently follow their ignorant politicians into hell, but not the people of the NFA. He had been more than happy to volunteer to deliver the bomb to the opera house.

To be chosen to light the fuse of Operation Thor was an honor greater than any others he could imagine. The modern world would label him a terrorist for his act, but future generations would call him a saint.

The man checked his watch and quickened his pace. Although he would reach the opera house with minutes to spare, he wanted to be well out of the vicinity when the explosive device went off. Its detonator was set for 10:00 A.M. The bomb had been programmed to do a limited amount of damage to the structure of the opera house and no more.

He turned and started up Circular Quay East to Bennelong Point. To his left was the Harbour Bridge, while directly ahead the millions of gleaming white tiles that decorated the opera house's geometric shells sparkled and danced beneath the winter morning sunshine.

Originally he was to enter the opera house by joining one of the complex's daily guided tours. This idea was vetoed after the NFA concluded that it would better suit their needs to have the bomb explode outside. Not that such details mattered to the man. Either way he was committed to doing his part in Operation Thor.

The forecourt of the opera house was packed with hundreds of foreign and local tourists admiring the country's most famous landmark. Couples strolled arm in arm. Whole families emerged from the numerous taxis depositing passengers at the site. The laughter of children and adults filled the air.

The man paused to take a quick photograph of the Harbour Bridge in the distance and then marched up the steps to the opera house's main entrance. Long lines were already forming for the next guided tour. The man continued past them and pressed on, ostensibly to gain a more favorable view of the harbour.

Finally he stopped and glanced from side to side as though searching for someone. Showing his disappointment, he unshouldered his camera case and lowered it to the ground. Dropping to one knee, he flipped open the case for a look inside. The postcards, film and Gregory's pocket map of Sydney were all doing fine.

So was the bomb.

He reclosed the case and stood, leaving it on the pavement. He rechecked his watch and realized that it was time to start back to the Circular Quay. He made a final show of scanning the rows of faces passing by him one last time, then shrugged slightly and began retracing his way to the forecourt.

"Excuse me, sir?" a voice unexpectedly called to him from behind.

The man suppressed a sharp intake of breath as he halted and turned around. *The police!*

The man drew the corners of his mouth into a tight-lipped smile. "Yes, Constable?"

"On holiday this morning are we, sir?" the man in the dark blue uniform questioned.

"I just arrived," the man lied. "Why do you ask? Have I done something wrong?"

The police constable grinned and shook his head. "Not at all. But you'll probably remember your visit to Sydney more fondly if you take your camera with you."

"Where's my head today?" The man touched his left shoulder. "I usually drape the strap right here and never take it off." He crossed back to the abandoned camera case and scooped it into his hand. "I'm pleased that one of us is awake. Thank you very much. I'm so embarrassed."

"No reason to be. Happens quite often really."

"Yes, well, thanks again."

"You're welcome, sir," the officer replied, then promptly walked away to continue his patrol of the area.

The man watched the policeman disappear. His feet were solid lead weights as he contemplated his next move. He knew that time was running out. Ten o'clock was less than five minutes away.

The man's brow beaded with sweat, and a cold chill of dread played games with his spine. What in hell was he going to do with the camera case and the bomb? Should he try to smuggle the bomb into the opera house after all? Even if he could, the long lines of tourists eliminated that option entirely.

He could walk to the edge of the harbour and throw the bomb into the water. That action would necessitate a twenty-four-hour delay in Operation Thor, but it would give the NFA the opportunity to carry out their plans exactly as intended. But there was always the possibility that by postponing Operation Thor for a day he might unintentionally create complications that could totally disrupt Nuclear Free Australia's hopes and dreams for world peace.

The man's eyes darted to the crystal of his digital watch. He had only three minutes and fifteen seconds. What was he going to do? A dozen options came and went in a flurry of desperation. Two minutes and thirty seconds to go. At this rate he would be sitting on top of the bomb when the damn thing exploded. Time was quickly running out. If Operation Thor was to continue as scheduled, there was only one option available to him.

Slipping the strap from his shoulder, he deposited the case on the ground again and began moving rapidly through the crowd toward the opera house forecourt. He could never make it back to Circular Quay before the explosion, but he could put some distance between himself and the bomb.

"This doesn't appear to be your day, does it, sir?" The police constable he had talked to earlier suddenly materialized directly in front of him, blocking his avenue of escape.

"What?" the man sputtered, wondering if he could outrun the policeman, then deciding he could not. "What's that?"

"Your camera case," the constable said, noting as he did the man's expression of anxiety. "That's the second time this morning you've left the case on its own, and that's hardly likely to be a coincidence. Let's go back and take a peek inside."

That would be suicide the man thought, bolting to his left and pushing aside a woman and her two children. Almost at once he felt the constable's fingers digging into his shoulders.

The man twisted, wriggling about like a fish impaled on a hook. He flailed his arms, trying to swing his fists into the constable's face. The officer blocked the attack and caught the man with a punch to the jaw.

The man screamed in pain as he spit blood and a single tooth from his mouth. Weakness overcame him, and his wildly swinging fists turned docile as he was forcibly hauled to his feet.

"I don't know what you're hiding in that camera case, mate," the policeman said, steering his captive through the throng of startled onlookers, "but if it's worth a beating, then I'm betting it's something you'd rather I not see."

The constable shoved the man against the side of the opera house building and ordered, "Stay put. I caught you once. I can catch you again."

"Wait," the man protested. "You don't under—"

"That will be all from you." The constable's fingers curled around the camera case's strap and pulled it into his arms. "Now, let's see what we—"

"We've got to run!" The man's voice cracked with fear while his eyes remained riveted to the grim object in the constable's arms.

Concern flickered across the lawman's face. "Run? What for?"

"Because there's a . . . there's a bomb in the case!"

The policeman opened his mouth to speak, but before he had a chance to utter a word the NFA bomb exploded, instantly killing both him and his prisoner in a burst of white-hot energy. Everyone within a radius of sixteen feet became a fatality statistic. Blood and body parts flew in every direction, striking tourists in a gory storm of horror as those not slaughtered by the fury of the bomb scattered in a dazed panic.

Within minutes the police arrived on the scene and immediately took charge of the situation. While a team of constables cordoned off the bomb site, other officers combed the crowds for reliable witnesses. Ambulances rushed the severely wounded victims to hospitals. Many of those suffering superficial cuts and scrapes were treated on the spot.

The experts from the bomb squad arrived and swept the area in a detailed search for additional explosives. When none was found, the green light was given to move in and sift through the rubble left by the NFA strike. The task was not a pleasant one. Fragments of bodies littered the ground like flesh and bone hailstones, including fingers, amputated limbs and a single severed head missing half of its face. One corpse lay sprawled with a coil of ropy intestines snaking from its ruptured belly. Blood dotted the pavement canvas in ugly splotches of varying sizes. Damage to the opera house itself was limited to an uneven hole gouged from the side of the structure.

Thirty minutes later most of the physical traces of the explosion had been removed. As the last of the fatalities was carted away, a senior inspector investigating the tragedy received a verbal report from one of the constables who had been on duty at the site.

"What do you have for me?" the inspector asked. "Any reliable information to be had?"

"Some, sir. Apparently, the man carrying the bomb was apprehended by one of our officers just prior to the actual explosion."

"Hmmm. Any idea as to the identity of the man we lost?"

"We believe it was a Constable Mayhill. Family man. Wife and two children."

"I want to be notified the second that information is confirmed," the senior inspector said. "His family will need to be told, and I'll be damned if they'll hear the news on the radio or television first."

"As soon as we know for sure it was Mayhill, I'll personally make it my responsibility to contact you, sir."

Terrorists, anarchists, hijackers and drug dealers—BEWARE!

In a world shock-tilted by terror, Mack Bolan and his courageous combat teams, *SOBs* and our new high-powered entry, *Vietnam: Ground Zero* provide America's best hope for salvation.

Fueled by white-hot rage and sheer brute force, they blaze a war of vengeance against a tangled international network of trafficking and treachery. Join them as they battle the enemies of democracy in timely, hard-hitting stories ripped from today's headlines.

Get 4 explosive novels delivered right to your home—FREE

Return the attached Card, and we'll send you 4 gut-chilling, high-voltage Gold Eagle novels—FREE!

If you like them, we'll send you 6 brand-new books every other month to preview. Always before they're available in stores. Always at a hefty saving off the retail price. Always with the right to cancel and owe nothing.

As a subscriber, you'll also get...
- our free newsletter *AUTOMAG* with each shipment
- special books to preview and buy at a deep discount

Get a digital quartz calendar watch—FREE

As soon as we receive your Card, we'll send you a digital quartz calendar watch as an outright gift. It comes complete with long-life battery and one-year warranty (excluding battery). *And like the 4 free books, it's yours to keep even if you never buy another Gold Eagle book.*

RUSH YOUR ORDER TO US TODAY.

have to wait in line like everyone else. "You probably know as much about the bombing as we do."

"I hope not," Bedford half laughed as he flicked the ash from his cigarette. "I'll be expecting the repairmen along any minute now. Will there be any problem getting them through the barriers to the building?"

"No problem at all, Mr. Bedford," Senior Inspector Harris promised. "Is there anything else you'll be needing, or are we free to continue with our investigation?"

"By all means, Inspector, don't let me interfere with your duties. The Ministry wants to get to the bottom of this terrible matter as quickly as possible, too. It doesn't do to have some madman blowing holes in our buildings, you know."

"Funny, I feel the same way about our citizens, Mr. Bedford, only most of those caught within range of the exploding bomb weren't as lucky as your building. They're beyond repair. Now, if you'll excuse me?"

"Certainly, Inspector Harris. And thank you again for you assistance."

Harris grumbled, then motioned for one of the constables to follow him.

Watching the two officers leave, George Bedford was privately pleased to have irritated the inspector so easily. It was obvious that Harris did not know how to show proper respect to true figures of authority. Bedford was not concerned. He had enough to think about without bothering himself with the personality deficiencies of a senior inspector.

Bedford turned to examine the hole in the opera house wall and was more than satisfied with what he saw. The shape of the hole was perfect; it would serve as a womb for the seed of a new age of peace that was soon to be born.

Within the hour the workmen would come and temporarily repair the hole, making it all but invisible to anyone standing in the opera house forecourt. But before they sealed it up, they would leave inside a present for the people of Sydney, a gift of salvation for the rest of the world.

The gift had traveled all the way from the United States. It weighed twenty-seven pounds.

20

An ASIO agent named Scott greeted McCarter, Manning and Lila Blake when they disembarked from their Ansett flight to Darwin. Scott identified himself to his female counterpart, then escorted her away from the others for a brief conference. As soon as the two Phoenix commandos were alone, David McCarter reached for the pack of Players in his pocket.

"Next time I pick the bleedin' seats," the Briton complained. "Not only does your girlfriend get to sit by the window, but we had to spend more than two hours in the air trapped in the no smoking section of the plane." He pulled a cigarette from the pack and brought the flame of a butane lighter to its tip. He inhaled deeply, then exhaled with a pleasurable sigh. "Oh, right. That's more like it. That's what life is all about."

"You were saying?" Manning coaxed, hoping to get McCarter's griping over before Lila returned.

"That next time we sit where I can smoke and I get the seat by the window."

"Those are tough demands, but I can live with them. Is that all?"

"For now. What's keeping Lila?"

"She's only been gone a minute."

"It seems like longer," the Englishman said impatiently.

"That's cause you're itching for a fight," Manning said. "You'll feel better after somebody has tried to shoot you or run you over."

McCarter brightened. "You think so?"

Manning held back his answer as Lila Blake appeared from around a corner. Agent Scott was nowhere to be seen. The expression on the Australian's face immediately told the Canadian that something was wrong.

"What's up?" Manning asked. "More trouble?"

"Yes," the woman answered. "While we were flying up here to Darwin, someone set off a bomb at the Sydney Opera House. There are seventeen confirmed fatalities, but the death toll is expected to rise."

"Do they know who planted the bomb?" McCarter asked.

Lila Blake shook her head. "The perpetrator was a male Caucasian whose estimated age was thirty-five. He died in the explosion, along with a police constable who was trying to arrest him. The other casualties happened to be in the wrong place at the wrong time."

"And after the blast there probably wasn't enough left of the bomber to scrape up with a knife," Manning guessed.

"Or of the constable," the woman added. "Obviously, the bomber made some mistake, or the constable would not have tried to arrest him."

"Any takers yet for the incident?" McCarter questioned.

"None," she said. "As far as we know the bomber was working solo."

"Then why was Agent Scott so secretive about it?" Manning asked.

"On the off chance the NFA was behind the explosion," Lila Blake continued. "ASIO thought I should be informed."

"What would a group calling itself Nuclear Free Australia have against the opera house?" Manning wondered.

"Have you ever sat through an opera?" McCarter inquired. "The lot of them sound alike, and all the good singers are built like oil tankers. But given the NFA's recent activities, plus their eagerness to admit their responsibility for crimes committed, it seems unlikely that they're tied in with the bombing."

"I agree," Lila Blake stated, "but for another reason. If the people belonging to the Nuclear Free Australia movement wanted to draw attention to themselves by bombing the Sydney Opera House, it's doubtful that they would have triggered the bomb at ten o'clock in the morning. I think the NFA would have waited until tonight."

"Tonight?" Manning repeated. "How do you mean?"

"There's an international trade conference going on in Sydney right now," she told him.

"Sure," the Canadian recalled. "Made up of nations belonging to the Commonwealth. They spoke about it briefly last night on the news. But what does a trade conference have to do with the opera house? I don't see the connection."

"Tonight there will be a benefit performance held at the opera house, and the trade representatives from the nations participating in the conference will be the guests of honor at the program."

"Which," McCarter concluded, "would have provided a much more likely time for the NFA to hit."

Lila Blake concurred. "Exactly. And that's why I think this morning's bombing attack is unrelated to our investigation. Nuclear Free Australia would have had better timing. And I'm not sure they would have used a bomb, although they certainly aren't opposed to violence. Their mandate seems to be full of contradictions."

"So, where's that leave us now?" Manning questioned.

"We pick up our gear," the woman said, "and then go outside where Scott is waiting for us. He'll be driving us into Darwin and acting as our guide while we're here."

"If Scott's going to be with us," McCarter said, "why couldn't he have told us about the bombing in Sydney?"

The ASIO agent smiled. "Scott doesn't know you boys like I do."

"I should bloody well hope not," Manning said as he walked toward the baggage pickup area.

When they had gathered all of their luggage, they moved outside to where Agent Scott was waiting in a Ford Falcon.

"So, what's a pommy bloke like you think of our fair land?" Agent Scott asked McCarter as they drove into Darwin. The Englishman sat in the front seat of the Falcon with Scott; Manning and Lila Blake rode in the back. "Did you ever see such a sight in all your life?"

McCarter studied the parched-looking land bordering the highway. "Only once," he confessed.

Scott was curious. "Where was that?"

"In the middle of a nightmare," McCarter said. "Is it always this arid?"

"Couldn't live here if it was," Scott told him. "We're still in what we call the Dry. Won't be into the Wet for another few weeks. That's when the Northern Territory comes to life. She's beautiful."

"Pity we won't get to see it," McCarter said, both he and Manning unpacking their weapons as Scott drove. "What about the people who were killed last night by the NFA?"

Scott's eyes shifted to McCarter, then back to the road. "What's to tell? They're all dead. And with the exception of the CIA operative, everyone died of multiple stab wounds. They looked like an ad for tomato sauce when we found them. The blood was everywhere except inside their bodies where it belonged."

"Was the same murder weapon used on all of the victims?" Manning asked from the rear.

"As near as we can tell," Scott said. "We reckon that whoever killed them has to be more than a bit unstable. Any one of the wounds suffered by the victims would have proved fatal. After that it was gravy. One poor man was stabbed a dozen times."

"And unless we find the killer and stop him," Lila Blake pointed out, "more innocent people will be murdered."

"So they promise," Scott said.

"Has anyone here ever heard of the Nuclear Free Australia movement before?" Manning asked.

Scott shook his head. "Not that we've been able to determine. If the NFA has been working in Darwin, they've kept their activities undercover. Then again, if there are only a few of the fanatics, it wouldn't be that difficult for them to maintain a low profile."

"Where do you suggest we go first?" Lila asked.

"The best place for us to start would most likely be the Botanical Gardens where the bodies were discovered," Scott said. "How's that sound?"

"Like music," McCarter said, speaking on behalf of the others.

"The gardens will almost make you forget the Dry," Scott promised. "They're right quiet and peaceful."

"I'M THIRSTY," one gunman said.

"So am I," another said. "Why don't we knock off for a while and get ourselves something to drink?

What do you say, Bromly? Fancy a drink to wash away the dust?''

"Even if I did, which I don't, it's out of the question," Davy Bromly answered. "We'll wait here for as long as it takes, so keep your complaints to yourself."

"How many of them are we expecting?" one of the killer's associates asked. He was a simple type. Big and strong. His weakest muscle was between his ears. "How many people do we get to kill?"

"I already told you," Bromly snapped. "There's two men and a woman."

"Is the sheila a looker?" the man beside Bromly asked.

"Who cares?" Bromly demanded. "All you need to know is that she's the enemy, and that when she and her friends finally arrive we hit the lot of 'em with everything we've got."

"Yeah," the man next to Bromly said. "No problem. But is the sheila a looker?"

Muttering something under his breath about morons, and caressing the submachine gun that rested across his lab, Bromly took a deep breath and restrained himself from cuffing the idiot against the side of his head.

Bromly had been informed by the NFA in Sydney that three troublemakers were on their way to Darwin. He was ordered to eliminate them. He was to utilize every available NFA member at his disposal to make certain that the visitors from the south did not survive their excursion north.

Bromly had questioned the need to involve the NFA members. "If there are only three agents coming to the Territory, I can handle them by my lonesome," he had told Ronald Thompson over the phone.

"Absolutely not," Thompson cautioned. "Trust me, Davy. You'll need help with these three."

"No way," Bromly protested. "You forget who you're talking to. I took care of the others last night on my own, didn't I?"

"Yes, you did. But these three will be different,"

"Yeah? How?"

"They'll be fighting back."

"We'll see. So, how many guns do I need?"

"Our records show an active membership of twenty individuals in Darwin."

"Sounds right. How many should I call upon to help me?"

"Use them all, Davy."

"I don't like it. You know I work alone."

"This time you don't," Thompson said. "In the end you'll be very glad that you listened to me."

Bromly had followed his orders and was now waiting outside Darwin's Botanical Gardens. The twenty Nuclear Free Australia gunmen were stationed at various locations within the property. In Bromly's book the entire business smacked of a cold slap in the face.

Whatever happened to confidence? Was Seb Hardy running scared all of a sudden? Bromly had no idea. He did know that, if push came to shove, the extra guns could lead to a first-class botch. Too many cooks spoil the broth, they said. Well, too many assassins could do the same with an otherwise uncomplicated hit. Bromly's only hope was that when the shooting started the three targets would accept their fate easily.

To make it easier for him to work without excessive interference, Bromly had deliberately positioned most of the NFA guns under his command at the opposite end of the gardens and as far away from the main entrance as possible. That way, he reasoned, he would have first crack at doing the job Seb Hardy wanted done. By the time the others got to the excitement, the party would be finished.

A Ford Falcon pulled into the lot across from where Bromly's car was parked. He tensed momentarily, then relaxed, his killer's sense instinctively telling him that his prey had arrived.

He squinted and watched as the Ford drove into an empty space and parked. The sedan's doors opened, and the vehicle's passengers climbed out, each openly carrying firearms.

"Hey, there's four of them," one of the brighter gunmen with Bromly noted immediately, proving that at least he could count. "How come there's not three?"

"The sheila's pretty, though," commented another of the NFA gunmen.

"Shut up and do what I tell you." Bromly affectionately stroked his SMG. "We've got work to do."

21

McCarter opened his door, swung his feet out of the car and got out. The incredibly dry air of Darwin instantly made the Briton crave an ice-cold glass of Coca-Cola Classic.

"How far into the gardens were the bodies discovered?" the Englishman wanted to know.

"We can walk there in a couple of minutes," Scott said, emerging from the Ford and stretching. "It will give you the chance to appreciate some of the scenery."

Manning climbed out of the Falcon and held the door open for Lila. "What about the area itself?" he asked. "Has it been cordoned off?"

"Yes," Scott told the Canadian. "We had orders not to reopen that section to the public until you had the opportunity to look it over."

"Good," McCarter said. "I'm sure ASIO did a bang-up job searching for clues, but we appreciate your thoughtfulness."

"As I said," Scott told the Cockney, "we were following orders."

Manning regarded the woman beside him. "And I wonder where those orders came from?"

The woman shrugged. "I wonder?"

"Right then," McCarter said. "To the gardens."

The British commando slammed the car door, and its window shattered, exploding into a shower of glass. A split second later the window on Gary Manning's door blew apart.

"Blimey!" McCarter shouted, swinging around with his Ingram MAC-10 just in time to see five NFA gunmen storm across the street in their direction.

One gunman, toting a silencer-equipped rifle, broke away from the rest of the group and attempted to bag the first kill of the day. McCarter had the same idea, aiming his Ingram and triggering a three-round burst of pure hell and destruction that burned through the killer's chest in a bloodied horizontal pattern. McCarter's bullets scored three in a row, and the gunman went down, flinging away his rifle and dropping with a thump to the pavement.

The next killer in line raised his submachine gun to fire, but a .357 Magnum-sized egg from Manning's Desert Eagle switched off the guy's lights forever. The perfectly aimed headshot bored through the bridge of the killer's nose and sprayed out the back of his skull, transforming the gunman into a leaking lump of useless flesh.

Scott dived over the hood of the Ford just as a stream of enemy slugs came stitching across his side of the car. Metal pinged and groaned as hot lead plowed into the auto's engine. Scott was sliding to safety when

McCarter reached out and grasped him by the shoulder, pulling the ASIO agent out of the NFA's direct line of fire.

"Thanks," Scott offered, crouching on the ground and bringing out his .38 S&W.

"You're welcome," McCarter said. "How about that tour of the gardens?"

"No time like the present," Scott agreed.

McCarter called to Manning, "You three head for the gardens while I cover you, then you can return the favor for me."

"Done," Manning said.

"Go!" McCarter yelled, making himself a target while Manning and the others beat a path to the gardens' primary entrance.

The Englishman's MAC-10 came alive, spitting out a wall of 9 mm terror that caught one advancing NFA killer in a diagonal blitz across the doomed gunman's midsection. Fire ravaged the thug's digestive organs. He emitted a shriek that few sopranos could duplicate and promptly sank to his knees to die.

Only two of the original five killers that McCarter had seen remained alive; both gunmen were doing their utmost to avoid the wave of Ingram bullets that were flying their way. Seeing this as an ideal chance to join the others, McCarter turned on his heels and charged for the entrance to the gardens. Almost immediately the NFA pair who were lying low were back on their feet giving chase.

McCarter was still twenty feet from his ultimate goal when he saw Manning and Lila Blake preparing to open fire in his direction. Instinctively, the battle-honed Briton dropped flat, giving his two colleagues a clean line of sight.

The big Canadian's .357 boomed in his fist, the Eagle's recoil traveling in reverse up his arm. Next to him, Lila Blake's .38 Police Special also got into the act, shots from both weapons permanently bringing down the curtain on the NFA killer who had been in the lead. The final gunman found refuge behind the bullet-riddled body of the Falcon.

McCarter jumped to his feet and dashed to where Manning and the two ASIO agents waited, angry slugs from the remaining killer nipping at the Londoner's heels every step of the way.

"Thanks," McCarter said as Manning helped him through the tree-shaded entrance to the gardens.

Scott unloaded a couple of shots, and the subgunner at the Ford ducked out of sight. "Ha! He's had it now. We've got the nong right where we want him. He can't go anywhere without exposing himself to our gunfire, and he can't get another shot at us unless he does. In short, the game's over."

A rifle cracked, and bark flew from the tree that Scott was using for cover. "Then again," he amended, "maybe not."

"Crikey!" McCarter swore. "You've got that one right, mate!"

Off to their right, less than twenty-five yards away, another half dozen NFA killers had materialized. They broke through the foliage at the forward boundary of the gardens. Racing for the garden's protected entrance like a pack of wolves lusting for blood, the six unwelcome additions to the NFA ranks all brandished automatic weapons.

The six gunmen began shooting simultaneously, determined to accomplish through sheer strength of numbers what their individual lack of accuracy could not achieve. Their strategy came close to succeeding. Criss-crossing the wooded entrance to Darwin's botanical wonderland, the intense barrage of bullets forced McCarter and the others to retreat farther into the gardens and prevented them from boldly resisting the attack.

But at least two of the six killers paid dearly for their beliefs. One Nuclear Free Australia flunky died when a .357 bolt of lightning from Manning's Eagle burst the loser's heart.

The second of the six NFA assassins literally bit the dust, catching a pair of Ingram rounds in a double dose of fire across his thighs. He reacted with a deep groan, losing his balance and stumbling across the garden. He dropped his weapon and clamped his palms over the twin holes that had been gouged from his legs. At that moment the saphenous vein of his inner right thigh burst open like a cheap balloon, sending a warm river of red over his fingers. Before his fate really registered, he was slamming into the ground face first, his mouth filled with the grittiness of dirt as he died.

The two Phoenix Force pros and their Aussie companions quickly retreated from the entrance and down a path that led farther into the gardens.

Replacing the M-10's magazine with a fresh one as they hurried along, McCarter turned to Scott. "Let me know when we come to that beautiful scenery that I'm supposed to appreciate."

DAVY BROMLY PICKED himself up off the ground and came running around the parked Ford Falcon that had saved his life. What a bleedin' botch up! Four NFA dead. No, make that six, he amended when he caught sight of two more bodies with faces that he recognized. All because that imbecile Peters had to start the fight before Bromly gave him the word. And what did Peters get for jumping the gun? A couple of smashed car windows and a lead-lined chest. Served the bastard right.

Bromly rushed up to the four numb-looking NFA gunmen standing at the entrance to the gardens.

"Where the hell are they?" Bromly shouted.

By way of an answer, one of Bromly's assistants jerked his thumb to the left. "They ran inside."

"Well then," Bromly fumed, his temper rising to a boil, "why aren't you chasing them? We're here to kill the scum, not to let them beat us in a foot race."

"We were waiting for you," one of the gunmen stammered.

"Get moving!" Bromly ordered, knowing fear when he heard it. "And no more games. I'll take pleasure in personally shooting the next one of you that lags behind. Move!"

Another gunman spoke up as he and the rest obeyed the command. "What happened to the men you were with, Davy?"

"The same bloody thing that will happen to you if you don't do as you're told," Bromly warned, prodding the curious NFA killer forward with the still-warm muzzle of his SMG.

From deep within the grounds of the gardens, an outburst of autofire suddenly disrupted the temporary lull in the battle.

"They've met up with the others," Bromly announced. "If we hurry it along we can trap the four between us!"

The five NFA men charged through the entrance to the gardens after their enemies, Davy Bromly thoughtfully bringing up the rear as he continually urged his men to greater speeds.

WHEN DAVID MCCARTER HAD ROUNDED a bend in the tree-lined trail, the British lion had been confronted by a group of Nuclear Free Australia gunmen running up the path toward him. The Cockney beat the killers to the draw, opening fire with his Ingram as the pack of fanatics scattered like a school of fish spooked by a shark.

Two of the NFA gunmen went down, three 9 mm zingers drilling a cavity of gloom in one killer's face. His features dissolved in a gusher of blood as the bullet-severed tip of his chin flew through the air.

More Ingram slugs carried a final message to the next NFA hoodlum in line. His life ended as he tried to run and gun down McCarter at the same time. He died without accomplishing either.

McCarter dived for the side of the trail and between the trunks of two trees to avoid being hit with NFA lead. Bullets bored holes in the bark as the Englishman scrambled for cover. Manning, Blake and Agent Scott were already using the trees for protection.

Manning and Scott fired their weapons and delivered another pair of killers to the gates of hell. Not to be outdone by her male counterparts, a sharp-eyed Lila Blake inflicted considerable damage on her own.

The ASIO female began by drilling a tidy hole in the forehead of a careless NFA gunman who showed too much face and not enough brains. Her next NFA target fared no better, exiting from life courtesy of a .38 slug that entered his chest through his rib cage and lodged in the right ventricle of his heart. The killer dropped his rifle to the ground and tried to dig the offending bullet from his wound. The finger sunk in blood to the first knuckle before death pulled him into a cold world of darkness.

Sensing movement out of the corner of his eye, McCarter spotted another wave of NFA gunmen creeping around the bend in the trail. "Everybody loves a party," he said to Manning.

An enemy bullet thudded harmlessly into the trunk of the tree Manning was behind as he noted, "They're part of the bunch we left at the front gate. Can you manage to bag a few of them?"

"Not without some unfriendly exposure to my right," McCarter answered.

Manning glanced over his shoulder, then looked to Scott. "What's in back of us?"

"Farther into the gardens is an amphitheater," Scott told him. "But we wouldn't get there without bullets chasing us every step of the way."

"Not if the NFA have something else to think about," the Canadian decided.

Lila Blake nudged Manning's side. "What do you have in mind, Gary?"

"A little game of hardball," Manning said.

Transferring his .357 Eagle to his left hand, Manning dipped his right into the Velcro-secured inner pocket of his jacket. When the hand reappeared, it contained two M-33 fragmentation grenades. Ball-shaped, 2.5 inches in diameter and weighing fourteen ounces, each of the olive drab M-33s had an effective frag range of just under fifty feet.

"We'll do it like this," Manning explained. "I throw, then we go." He said to Scott. "Since you're our tour guide, you get to lead us to the amphitheater. Lila will follow next."

"What about you two?" the Australian woman asked.

"Don't worry about us," Manning assured her. "Just keep running until you reach the amphitheater. We'll follow, and it may pay to have you there ahead of us to offer cover fire if we need it. Everybody ready?"

Everybody was. The six NFA members directly opposite them presented the greatest potential danger as they were so close to where Manning and his companions were positioned. For this reason, Manning elected to toss the first M-33 at them. He set one grenade on the ground then, holding down the safety lever of the second M-33, turned to look at Lila Blake.

"How about pulling my pin?" he asked.

The woman smiled. "Thought you'd never ask," she said, performing the requested task. "I expect to see you at the amphitheater."

"And you won't be disappointed," Manning promised.

The M-33 has a delay element that burns from four to five seconds before triggering its detonator. The delay allows the thrower enough time to heave the M-33 up to 132 feet before it explodes.

Manning cocked his arm back and let the grenade fly. It soared over the trail and landed directly in front of a pair of startled NFA men. The ball-shaped bomb bounced and rolled between the dumbstruck duo as they reacted to the M-33's unexpected arrival by trying to run in opposite directions. Neither managed more than a few frantic steps before the grenade erupted, the preengraved frag ripping through fabric and flesh in a furious flash of raw energy. With blood soaking the backs of their shirts, the two NFA gunmen were lifted off their feet, dead from the shock of the blast before they hit the ground.

The noise of the explosion still hung in the air when a NFA assassin nearby suddenly screamed and jumped into view, both his hands clawing madly at the hollow sockets of his eyes. Blood flowed through his fingers as he ran blindly onto the trail. McCarter ended the man's suffering with a double dose of Ingram lead.

BROMLY'S FIRST IMPULSE was to turn tail and hide when the grenade exploded. Instead, his courage bolstered by the four NFA men in front of him, the subgunning killer shouted at his stunned troops.

"Don't stand there like idiots!" he hollered. "They're ahead of us behind the trees!"

Bromly fired a three-round burst to get his men going, and that did the trick. Galvanized by the very real threat of being gunned down by their own leader, the four NFA shooters swallowed their fear and attacked just as Manning's second M-33 came rushing through the air straight toward them.

Bromly saw the grenade first and reacted accordingly, flattening himself to the trail and covering the top of his head with his arms. His four obedient followers were not so fortunate.

Landing squarely on the boots of one of the advancing NFA killers, the M-33 erupted with a mighty roar. The boot nearest the explosion was blown off; so was the foot trapped inside it. The owner took one quick glimpse at the bloody stump of his leg and then died of shock.

One killer lost both his breakfast and the stomach containing it as shrapnel tore apart his gut. The gunman beside him had his jugular sliced and spent the final seconds of his life trying to stop the warm red flow of life, while the final NFA hit man to confront the full fury of the grenade caught a barrage of burning metal in his chest. A fist of nails squeezed his heart in an iron grip, and a sticky liquid bubbled up his throat. The man collapsed and fell on the bodies of his fallen comrades.

The noise of the explosion faded, and Bromly uncovered his head. A sharp stinging sensation above his left elbow told him that he had been hit, but the wound was superficial. Not like the wounds inflicted on the rest of his men. Bromly's face blanched, turning the color of white bread when he saw what remained of the four NFA gunmen sprawled on the trail before him. All of the four were dead. Only he had survived.

Hearing the sounds of renewed gunfire up ahead, Bromly climbed to his feet and rushed forward, fiercely determined to kill his enemies, even if he was killed in the process.

Agent Scott and Lila Blake were up and making tracks for the amphitheater the moment Manning's second grenade started to reduce the opposition to NFA mincemeat. A lone killer across the trail saw them fleeing and boldly stepped into the open to bring the pair down. He was raising his pistol to fire when McCarter and Manning zeroed in on his position with a wave of destruction from their respective weapons.

Three Magnum-sized eggs from Manning's Eagle and a half dozen of McCarter's 9 mm MAC-10 mini-rockets jerked the marksman across the trail. Supported by the shock waves of bullets striking his flesh, the NFA goon finally surrendered to gravity and met the earth with outstretched arms.

Manning and McCarter ceased fire and turned to follow the ASIO agents hurrying for the amphitheater. Both Phoenix Force pros kept low as they ran to minimize their target potential.

Suddenly, none of that mattered as two battle-crazed NFA killers crashed through the foliage in a final assault. The first of the pair perished when one of Manning's .357 slugs found a home between the man's eyes, but before the Canadian could dispatch the next NFA savage the man was upon him with a growl like that of a caged beast.

A physical brute, the remaining killer slammed into Manning like a runaway truck. He bowled the Canadian over and sent the Eagle pistol flying from Manning's hand. A rock-hard fist connected in a glancing blow off the side of the Phoenix warrior's jaw.

The brawny Canadian grunted and filed the pain in the back of his mind. Survival had to remain foremost in his thoughts. Another punch zoomed at him. Manning caught the wrist behind the descending fist with his left hand and drove a powerful right uppercut under the terrorist's rib cage. He stepped forward and placed a hip against the larger man's buttocks as he reached around and grabbed the stunned man's shirt front. Manning's shoulders pivoted, and he bent his knees to send his opponent hurling backward over his hip.

The NFA goon crash-landed, and Manning kicked him in the solar plexus. The terrorist moaned, and

Manning launched another kick aimed at the big man's skull. Hands suddenly snared Manning's boot. A twist threw the Canadian off balance, and he tumbled to the hard ground.

The killer staggered to his feet as Manning scrambled upright. The Aussie hulk lunged, both arms extended as if he was trying to imitate a Frankenstein monster in a cheap horror film. Manning dodged the clumsy attack and drove a fist into the guy's hard abdomen. He followed with a left and then a solid right to the Aussie's chin. It was like duking it out with a bag of cement. Manning knew his punches landed because his fists stung from the impact. Yet his opponent stayed on his feet. He seemed to be getting stronger.

"You're dead, mate," the Aussie promised. He lowered his head and charged, right fist swinging toward Manning's midsection.

The Phoenix fighter stepped away, narrowly avoiding the NFA killer's blow. The killer's head was still tucked low, so Manning swung his foot and kicked the man in the face as hard as he could. The Australian's back straightened, and his head snapped upward. Manning hit him with an overhead right, smashing his knuckles into the terrorist's nose.

The killer howled as blood flowed from his crushed nose. He bellowed with rage and snorted; the action caused a gooey spray of blood and mucus to spurt from his semiclosed nostrils. Manning stepped forward and kicked his opponent in the lower abdomen. The thug groaned and bent slightly.

Manning feinted another kick. The brute reached out to try to grab a boot that did not swing forward. He left his face unprotected, and Manning swiftly scored another punch on the terrorist's shattered nose. The man howled with pain and staggered backward, swaying unsteadily.

The Canadian slammed a fierce side kick at the hulk's kneecap. Bone grated in the joint, and the big man tumbled on all fours. Manning clasped his hands together, raised his arms and hammered the doubled fists into the nape of his opponent's neck. Vertebrae cracked, and the man slumped face first on the ground.

Davy Bromly arrived at the scene as Manning checked to make sure the Aussie was dead. The murder expert smiled thinly as he set his sights on Manning's broad back and prepared to deliver the final blow.

Blue-black steel flashed, and a hard object struck the submachine gun from Bromly's hands. His arms tingled painfully from finger to shoulder. Bromly saw David McCarter's face briefly before the British commando clipped the NFA hit man across the chin with the noise suppressor attached to the barrel of his MAC-10. Bromly's teeth gnashed together and bit off the tip of his tongue. He spit the piece from his mouth.

"Easy, bloke," McCarter warned. "Unless you want the ants snacking on your brains."

"Pommy bastard," Bromly swore, lisping slightly because of his damaged tongue.

"Sticks and stones, mate," McCarter said with a shrug. Then he suddenly stabbed the muzzle of his silenced Ingram into the assassin's midsection.

Bromly doubled up, but he caught McCarter's MAC-10 with his left hand and shoved it toward the sky as a three-round burst erupted from the weapon. Simultaneously, Bromly's free hand streaked beneath his coat for the knife that he always carried. The deadly blade sprang into view.

Bromly attacked with an inside slash that came within a fraction of an inch of exposing McCarter's internal organs to the elements. Instinctively, the Briton pulled away. Sunlight glinted against the six-inch steel blade. The razored edge of the knife found the fabric of the Londoner's jacket and easily ripped through the material. McCarter sucked in his already iron-hard gut as the cold steel of the blade swept by.

McCarter had to release the Ingram to avoid another knife slash. Bromly heaved the MAC-10 overhead, holding it by the silencer-shrouded barrel. The killer smiled at McCarter as he waved the knife toward the Briton's face. McCarter considered the odds of backing away and drawing his Browning Hi-Power from its shoulder leather before the assassin could shish kebab him with the knife point. They were not very good, he realized.

Bromly raised the knife for another stroke, but then suddenly swung the Ingram like a hammer. The butt of the pistol grip struck McCarter on the right shoulder. The Briton grunted and staggered from the blow as Bromly lunged toward McCarter with his knife.

The British ace sidestepped, and the knife narrowly missed the right side of his rib cage. McCarter snap-kicked his opponent in the gut. Bromly gasped and delivered a vicious knife sweep. Again the Englishman's evasive actions saved his life. He jumped clear of the blade.

Bromly snarled and swung the Ingram like a war club. This time McCarter was ready. His boot lashed a solid kick to the killer's wrist, and the MAC-10 was hurled from numb fingers. Bromly furiously lunged, aiming his knife at McCarter's throat.

The Phoenix professional held his ground as the knife descended. His left hand suddenly chopped against Bromly's wrist at the last possible moment. Hooking his right arm under Bromly's arm, McCarter's hand grasped his opponent's wrist above the knife.

Using this figure-four hold to his advantage, McCarter exerted pressure on the NFA killer's limb and was rewarded when the arm gave out with a satisfying crack. The arm bent at an odd angle, and McCarter directed the blade down and in, pushing the knife deep into Bromly's abdomen.

Bromly gasped in agony and doubled up as McCarter allowed him to fall. The Briton stepped back and drew his Browning. Although wounded, the NFA assassin was still dangerous, and McCarter did not intend to take any chances with the bastard. He snapped off the safety catch and aimed the Browning at Bromly.

"Doc...doc...doctor," Bromly groaned. His mouth worked in strange shapes as he thrashed upon the ground, a painful fire engulfing his belly. "Get me to...a hospital."

"My pleasure," McCarter said. "But first you're going to tell me what I want to know."

"Any...thing," Bromly lisped through clenched and bloodied teeth. "What?"

"I want to know about the NFA," McCarter explained. "Somebody is king of the garbage mound. Probably the son of a bitch who hired you. I want to know his name."

"Don't know any NFA," Bromly lied.

"Then what good are you?" McCarter said with a shrug. "Just tell me who hired you. What point is there in protecting him now? Is he worth bleeding to death for?"

"No!" Bromly coughed as a spasm tore through his system. "Leader of NFA...his name...Har... Har...Har..."

"Bloody idiot," McCarter muttered as he watched Bromly's body relax in the final stillness of death.

"You questioning a captive?" Manning asked as he approached.

"I'd just be talking to myself if I tried now," McCarter replied. "Which is pretty much what I was doing before he kicked off anyway."

"Didn't tell you anything?" the Canadian said, frowning.

"Not much," the Briton said with a shrug as he returned his Browning to shoulder leather. "What about that bloke you had the donnybrook with?"

"I guess I hit him too hard," Manning answered. "He's dead. I don't suppose you managed to spare any of the rest of these human maggots?"

"Sort of hard to do," McCarter remarked. "I take it you had to kill all the Aussies who came at you, too."

"Yeah," Manning confirmed. "And with them goes any information we might have learned concerning the Nuclear Free Australia Movement. Wonderful."

22

The stocky terrorist was either too dumb to quit or too crazy to die. His right arm hung useless, shattered at the shoulder by a .45 caliber slug. Yet he charged toward Calvin James with his left hand arched in a claw. The black commando did not want to kill him. He held his fire, hoping the psycho would either faint or surrender.

The fanatic did neither. He suddenly swung a roundhouse kick. His boot struck the Colt Commander from James's fist. The terrorist hooked a solid left at the black warrior's jaw, sending James staggering toward the open barbecue pit. Fierce heat caressed James, warning him that the coals at the bottom of the trench were still burning.

"Shit," James rasped as he moved away from the pit.

The terrorist blocked James's path. The NFA lunatic's eyes burned with the hatred and zeal of an extremist, one who was willing to die for his chosen cause and very eager to kill for it. He raised his left fist and launched another wild punch at the black man's face.

James parried the punch with an outside forearm block and hooked a kick to the maniac's ribs. The terrorist staggered past James, turned sharply and prepared to charge. The Phoenix pro snapped a short kick at the guy's groin with his right foot. The terrorist swung a hand low to protect himself before he realized the kick was a feint. James's left foot delivered the real attack, a high tae kwon-do kick to the face that sent the man reeling backward . . . right over the edge of the barbecue pit.

The fanatic screamed as flesh sizzled and hissed on the metal grill stationed above the bed of white-hot coals. The terrorist shrieked and tried to rise, fingers and palms erupting with blisters that formed and popped with bloody steam. Tendrils of smoke curled around the screaming man's clothes, and he ignited into flames.

The terrible sweet stench of burning flesh quickly filled the air. Yakov Katzenelenbogen finished the dying man off with the aid of his Uzi, the mercy rounds stitching across the target's chest and into his heart. The dead man twitched as the Israeli's bullets struck home. Lifelessly, the corpse slipped to the floor of the pit.

Getting to The Resort on Dunk Island had been easy for the Stony Man warriors. The hard part was in trying to live long enough to unpack their bags. The man who Katz had just killed had attacked before the Phoenix commandos could even begin to cook something for lunch.

The three men returned to their cabana and began discussing their next move. But before they had finalized any of their plans the decision was made for them.

Katz spotted two gun-wielding NFA killers just as they prepared to fire from the sliding glass doors at the side of the room. Unfortunately for the eager assassins, the Israeli commando already had his Uzi in hand and automatically put it to work.

Shouting for his friends to keep down, Katz opened fire, blasting apart the glass doors with a storm of 9 mm lead. The two gunmen did not stand a chance. One of the killers actually succeeded in firing his weapon before he died, but the damage was limited to plowing up the sand surrounding a nearby palm tree.

A hasty examination outside determined that the NFA hit men had apparently launched their attack on their own. However, knowing that the sound of shooting was certain to attract the wrong kind of attention, Katz and the others elected to abandon their cabana.

Their weapons in tow, the elite counterterrorists were just leaving when the first real contingent of NFA killers came running around a curved row of rooms. Immediately, the band of fanatics recognized their quarry and made a full-scale assault.

Utilizing a stance that reflected all of Hollywood's cop shows, one gunman fired his rifle from the hip. The wasted shot went high and to the right, slamming into the rooftop of a distant cabana. Before the rifleman could correct his aim, Karl Hahn stopped him dead with a triple helping of H&K lead.

Gone before anyone around him realized it, the slain NFA hoodlum stumbled and slumped to his knees. A second killer tripped over the body and sprawled to the ground, opting to remain there forever when three bullets from Hahn's MP-5 cracked apart the assassin's skull.

Katz and company left one set of pursuers behind only to trade them for another as they rounded the next corner of the building. The two groups met in an open area adjacent to the sparkling waters of the complex's swimming pool. Legitimate guests at the resort scattered for cover.

Knowing they would be trapped between two groups of NFA hit men unless they worked quickly, the three Phoenix soldiers lost no time in dealing with their enemies. They were aided by the fact that the five gunmen were standing too close together to properly use their weapons.

It was a sobering lesson that one NFA killer learned when Calvin James erased most of the loser's face with a single decisive shot from his Colt Commander. The thunderous report of the Colt lived longer than Calvin's target did. Brain matter and blood sprayed from the exit wound as the target's warm corpse toppled to the stone patio surrounding the pool.

Wiping the gory mess from his face, a second NFA savage reopened his eyes to a sight that he would remember for the rest of his life. That life ended a heartbeat later when the Colt Commander that James was holding only an inch from the man's baby blues suddenly fired.

While James was keeping busy, Karl Hahn eliminated a third NFA hood with a blipping series of H&K manstoppers. But before he could cut down killer number four, his potential target leaped over the body of Hahn's first victim, slamming into the West German with a bone-jarring tackle. Hahn's MP-5 slipped from his fingers, dangling uselessly by its nylon lanyard as the two men hit the patio. The NFA tough worked the side of his rifle under Hahn's chin and began pressing down.

Hahn braced his palms against his opponent's weapon and pushed in an effort to prevent the Aussie hit man from choking him to death. Leverage and gravity were in the NFA killer's favor, however, as he leaned forward and exerted additional weight on his rifle. The maneuver worked.

Hahn's arms bent at the elbows, and the slowly descending rifle drew dangerously nearer to its goal. Hahn's eyes bulged and his temples pulsed with rage. The German commando felt the edge of the rifle settle upon his throat just as he noticed a pen clipped to his enemy's breast pocket. Holding back the rifle with his left hand, Hahn's right flew out from beneath the gun and grabbed the ballpoint. The killer had only registered what was happening when Hahn stabbed the pen into the side of the NFA goon's neck.

"God!" the killer gasped in a bellow of pain.

Hahn withdrew the pen and stabbed again, this time driving its point into the hollow of his adversary's throat. Blood spurted over his fingers as he drove the pen deeper and left it there.

Screaming at the top of his lungs, the man released the rifle and rose to his feet, his right hand trying to pull the imbedded pen free. His fingers closed on the object, but at first the pen was too slippery to grip.

Desperate, the man tore a strip of cloth from his shirt and used that to grab onto the pen. Hahn made no move to stop him. When the pen was finally yanked free, blood gushed from the unplugged wound. The man's screams became gurgles as he twisted on his feet and tripped over one of the poolside lounge chairs. With his fingers still trying to stem the flow of blood from his neck, the killer lost his balance and fell into the swimming pool. A pink cloud of death followed him all the way to the bottom of the pool.

The fifth and final NFA assassin thought he could easily polish off Katz, a fatal misconception that evaporated in a hellish squeal after the killer felt the Israeli's three-pronged prosthesis rip into his gut. Katz's would-be executioner doubled over into a ball of pain and died.

While James assisted Hahn to his feet, Katzenelenbogen reacted to the sound of rapidly approaching footsteps, obviously belonging to the NFA survivors of the brief gunfight outside their cabana. The Israeli aimed his Uzi in the appropriate direction and began to count, getting to five before the first of the eager NFA killers came charging around the corner and into sight. Katz fired, dusting his grim-faced foe across the chest. The remaining NFA hit men turned on their heels and got the hell out of the Phoenix commander's aim.

The three Phoenix professionals found themselves back on the beach and not far from the open barbecue pit. But before they could make it safely behind the pit's protective white brick wall, they were attacked by two NFA men who had not joined the group's main offensive. Katz and James scored perfect shots before either of the gunmen could react to the return of the Phoenix Force commandos.

"I don't like it," James said, taking advantage of the lull in the fighting to reload. "Despite those last two stragglers, it's just too quiet. Those stubborn bastards are up to something. Our tour guide is going to hear about this, let me tell you."

"Do you think Gary and David got the same kind of reception in Darwin?" James asked.

The Israeli colonel nodded as he inserted a fresh magazine into his Uzi. "Most definitely. We've been a thorn in the NFA's backside since we arrived in Sydney. They want us dead."

"And they aren't too particular about how many of their own people they lose in the process," Hahn observed. "Whatever they are trying to protect is obviously very important to the Nuclear Free Australia movement."

"Well, whatever it is," James said, "it's not something here on Dunk Island."

"Or in Darwin, for that matter," Katz concluded. "No, the answer to whatever the NFA has up its dirty sleeve waits for us in Sydney."

"That settles it then," James cheerfully announced. "All we need to do is wrap up our business here and be on our way. So, who wants to break the news to the NFA? I'm sure they'll listen to reason."

"And if they don't," Katz lifted his Uzi, "we'll resort to a little diplomacy."

"A bit late for that, I'm afraid," Hahn noted. "it doesn't appear that our opponents are in much of a talkative mood."

James and Katz visually confirmed what Hahn already knew. Having earlier failed to destroy the Phoenix Force trio, the remaining six Nuclear Free Australia gunmen had separated to launch a coordinated attack from both sides of the barbecue pit. Three killers appeared to the left of the Stony Man crew, three more to the right. Simultaneously, the gunmen opened fire.

Being the object of attention for a half dozen gun-happy killers was not the most comforting thing in the world, but Katz and his associates had been down that road before. Previous experience had shown time and again that the best course of action was to lower the odds as quickly as possible—a tactic the Phoenix team was quite prepared to employ.

With enemy lead scattering the sand at their feet, and digging uncomfortably large holes from the brick wall barricade, the men of Phoenix Force fearlessly met their antagonists' final gambit.

Katz fired to the left. Hahn took the right, while a deadly serious James switched back and forth between the two. One NFA hood died almost instantly with a bellyful of Uzi lead. Katz selected his next target, and with great precision bagged another hostile NFA goon a second later. The third killer on the left was dumped on his ass thanks to a pair of Colt persuaders from James.

Karl Hahn's accuracy with his MP-5 was equally as deadly, the former GSG-9 agent slaying two NFA triggermen with back-to-back headshots. Only one NFA piece of trash was left on his feet—a stocky runt with reddish hair and a beard to match. In the man's hand was a S&W Model 629 revolver.

James took aim with his Colt and shouted, "Drop your weapon or I'll shoot!"

But the gunman kept on coming, running even faster after hearing James speak. The killer was twenty-five feet from the barbecue pit when he finally raised his .44 Magnum.

The Colt Commander barked twice in quick succession, both of its missiles delivering a salvo of oblivion to the solo NFA gunner. The hit man's revolver spilled to the sand, and so did its owner.

When he was at last convinced that the conflict was over, Katz signaled that it was safe to go out into the open. "That's the lot of them," he said. "And they say diplomacy is a thing of the past."

A helicopter swept over their position and came in for a landing on the beach. The Phoenix pros tensed, unsure whether or not the chopper contained NFA reinforcements. Once the chopper's passengers disembarked, however, they were able to relax their guard.

"How was Darwin?" Katz inquired as Manning, Lila Blake and David McCarter approached.

"Not too much different than here, judging from the looks of things," Manning replied. "We hopped a ride over because we thought something like this might happen."

"It's a bitch being right all the time," James commented.

"Did you take any prisoners?" McCarter asked.

Katz shook his head. "The NFA fought us to their last man."

23

The representatives attending the trade conference for Commonwealth nations sat down to dinner at precisely 6:30 P.M. The Bennelong was famous for its fine cuisine as well as for its panoramic views of Sydney Harbour and of the magnificent city itself.

Ninety minutes had been allotted for the meal, after which time the Commonwealth representatives and their hosts would leave for the Concert Hall of the Sydney Opera House. The evening's benefit program was to be performed by the Sydney Symphony Orchestra. The Concert Hall seated 2,700, and a full house was expected. Tickets for the concert had been sold out in less than an hour. Anticipation for the program ran high.

The diners at the Bennelong Restaurant savored their food, sampled the Australian wine and renewed friendships from the past. They did all of these things without realizing that the biggest event of the evening had absolutely nothing to do with the dinner or the opera house and Sydney's Symphony Orchestra.

THE JET CARRYING PHOENIX FORCE and Lila Blake was scheduled to touch down at Kingsford Smith Airport at seven o'clock. The group had arrived at Cairns from Dunk Island after the last daily flight back to Sydney had taken off. Lila Blake put her considerable ASIO clout to work and had arranged to have a Boeing 727 fly them south.

A half hour outside of Sydney, Lila Blake had been summoned into the cockpit to receive a radio transmission from ASIO. When she returned to the group, she was carrying a sheet of paper covered with notes.

"What's the news?" Manning wanted to know.

She held out the piece of paper. "It's the list of names we requested of the present and former members of the Nuclear Disarmament Party who have sufficient funds to bankroll an organization like the NFA."

Katz looked over the list. "Ten names. Do any of these people have a reputation for participating in radical activities to support their antinuclear beliefs?"

"No," she said as the Israeli passed the list to McCarter. "Their only link to the Nuclear Free Australia movement at this stage of the game is that each person listed could probably afford to finance an NFA-type group if they wanted to."

"What about him?" McCarter interrupted, excitedly pointing to one of the names appearing on the list.

Lila Blake read off the name in question. "Sebastian Hardy. He's an extremely wealthy Sydneysider.

Made his fortune in uranium. Why, does his name ring a bell?''

"I don't know," McCarter confessed. "Remember the geezer at the Botanical Gardens in Darwin, the one I said died laughing?"

"Sure," the woman replied. "He wound up stuck on his own knife."

"That's the one," the Briton confirmed.

"He told you something?" Hahn asked.

"Maybe he did," McCarter said. "When I asked him to tell me the name of the NFA's leader, all I got out of him was 'har-har-har.' At the time I thought he was toughing it out, taking the piss right to the end. Could be I was wrong."

"And now you think he really might have been trying to give you this Hardy dude's name?" James concluded.

"Why not?" McCarter said, shrugging. "If he thought telling me what I wanted to know was going to save his hide, then, yeah, he could have been leveling with me just before he croaked."

"If that's the case, we'll soon find out," Katz said.

"What about the round-the-clock surveillance we had put on C. L. Roberts?" Manning inquired, referring to the Nuclear Disarmament Party member who had aroused their suspicions the day before. "Is he behaving himself?"

"So far," the ASIO agent told the Canadian. "Roberts went to his office as usual today, and at last check had returned home. He hasn't done anything out of the ordinary."

"Perhaps he's just going through the motions of a typical day because he knows he's being watched," Hahn guessed.

"Or maybe he didn't have anything to do with the NFA in the first place," Manning reluctantly suggested. "But if he really is clean, then yours truly is slipping. I could swear that guy was holding back on me when I visited him. After I asked him about the three missing CIA men, old C.L. got real defensive and jumpy."

"How long will ASIO maintain the surveillance?" Katz questioned.

"Indefinitely," Lila Blake answered. "After the trouble we encountered in Darwin and on Dunk Island, my government is more anxious than ever to see this operation brought to a close. The five of you seem to know what you're doing, which is why ASIO has been ordered to continue assisting you in any capacity you deem necessary."

The captain of the flight signaled that it was time to buckle their seat belts as they began their descent into Sydney.

"What's our plan when we land?" Manning asked Katz.

The Israeli's mouth went dry as the jet lost altitude. "It might not be a bad idea for us to pay this Sebastian Hardy fellow a visit. If Hardy is the money behind the NFA, then it's up to us to shut down his bank for good."

Several minutes later they were on the ground and taxiing to a special location on the runway. They would be able to leave the jet and the airport without having to fight the passenger traffic from the commercial flights that would crowd the terminal.

As they climbed down the steps of a portable metal ramp, Lila Blake was met by one of her colleagues from ASIO. She conferred with him briefly, then he walked to one of the automobiles parked near their 727 and drove off.

Phoenix Force gathered around her as she spoke to Manning, speaking loudly in order to be heard over the roaring engines of a jumbo jet that was preparing to take off.

"You're not slipping up, Gary," she said. "It looks as if you were right about C. L. Roberts. He is tied in somehow with the NFA."

"Good," Manning said, sounding relieved. "How do we know that?"

"The ASIO surveillance team assigned to cover him just called in to report that Roberts left his home a short while ago and took a little drive."

"Oh?" Manning wondered. "Anywhere in particular?"

Lila Blake nodded. "He drove to see Sebastian Hardy."

24

Sebastian Hardy could still taste the *Zampino* he had eaten at lunch despite the fact he was now eating dinner. The large man took a swallow of chilled mineral water and then picked up his fork and stabbed himself another piece of boiled wild rabbit. The tempting stuffing of blended ox kidneys, veal fat, and sandwich bread soaked in milk made the meal another of Hardy's favorites.

Hardy was amazed that he could eat at all under the circumstances. Davy Bromly was dead. So was Arthur French. Sydney's radio stations had been carrying the news of the Darwin and Dunk Island gunfights since late afternoon. More than forty people had perished in the two battles, and what riled Hardy the most was the apparent fact that all of the casualties had been NFA members.

"Thank God we lured the bastards north," Hardy had told Cheswick when they had received the bad news. "If we had let that rabble from America remain here in Sydney, it might have been us they're talking about now on the radio instead of Bromly and French."

Hardy was devouring his rabbit in the private dining area of his house where he ate whenever the cares of the world got him down. Furnished with a hardwood table, crystal chandelier and a chair specifically constructed to support his weight, the room had rarely been used in the last five years.

The last time Hardy had dined alone in the room was after the plumbers had come to his home to install customized toilets with extra-wide seats. Hardy was so depressed over the incident that he had almost skipped his second supper.

Reflecting on it now, Hardy would have gladly accepted a million visits from the plumbers if they would have saved him from having his nose repeatedly rubbed in the dirt by his enemies. Still, the interfering meddlers *were* up north and, ultimately, that was all that mattered. Operation Thor would proceed as planned and, within the next few hours, Nuclear Free Australia would show the world where it was headed. The NFA would activate the weapon it considered to be the greatest threat to man's survival; it would remind the world of the destruction caused by a nuclear weapon.

A light tapping sounded on the door to Hardy's right. He shoveled another mouthful of stuffing down his throat before responding.

"It's unlocked," he said.

The door opened noiselessly, and Cheswick entered the room.

"You know I'm eating, Lawrence," Hardy said. "Why are you disturbing me? Haven't I suffered enough grief for one day?"

"Forgive me, Sebastian," Cheswick apologized, "but I knew you would want to be informed when all of our guests had arrived. It's almost seven, and since this evening's draw was scheduled to begin at six, I—"

"All right. All right. I get the point." Hardy lowered his fork to his plate and motioned for Cheswick to step forward and untie his bib. "How's everyone feeling tonight, Lawrence?"

"Quietly reserved," Cheswick said.

"Reserved? About what?"

"There's some concern about the effect that our failures in the north will have on Operation Thor."

"Is that so?" Hardy said smugly.

"Yes, Sebastian." Cheswick undid the bib and moved aside as Hardy's chair glided away from the table on a silent cushion of compressed air. "In fact, some of the members have even suggested that we postpone Operation Thor until this all blows over."

"That will be Thompson's work," Hardy guessed correctly, activating a button on the control console in the arm of his chair. The chair's automatic internal hydraulic system raised both the seat and Hardy's enormous backside at the same time. When the seat reached its summit, it tilted and deposited Hardy's feet firmly on the floor. "I've never made an issue of it, of course, but Thompson is gutless. I'm sure he's afraid of the sight of blood.''

Hardy dipped his meaty hand into the voluminous pocket of his smoking jacket and retrieved a dozen chocolate after-dinner mints filled with cherry liqueur. He ate four of them at once and then continued.

''I hold Thompson personally responsible for the massacres at Darwin and Dunk Island. If Bromly and French weren't the men for the job, then Thompson should have realized that and hired more capable people. And now the idiot is talking about delaying Operation Thor? Why, that's tantamount to treason. Mutiny, that's what it is. If we weren't so close to finally realizing Operation Thor, I would seriously consider placing Ronald Thompson in front of an NFA firing squad. That would make the beggar sing a different tune!''

''I agree,'' Cheswick quickly offered as he and Hardy started for the door. ''Of course, Sebastian, you could obtain the results you want without all of that aggravation.''

Hardy smiled, biting into another mint. ''Yes, I like that. One of us must visit the opera house tonight. Why not Ronald Thompson?''

''But in order for that to happen,'' Cheswick indicated, ''Thompson would have to be the winner of our draw.''

Hardy laughed. ''Perhaps this is his lucky night.''

If the remaining Nuclear Free Australia members had expected Hardy to bemoan the fact that the NFA movement had once again been beaten by its enemies, they were sorely disappointed when their leader finally put in his appearance. Conversing amicably with Cheswick, and chuckling over some private joke, Hardy entered the room and made his way to the head of the conference table as though he had nothing more on his mind than which set of cutlery to use for his next meal.

Cheswick pulled out Hardy's chair for him, and Hardy settled down on the leather seat like a hippo sinking into mud. The obese Australian ate a chocolate mint, and then beaming like an advertisement for new dentures, called the evening's meeting to order.

"My friends," Hardy began, "we are gathered here tonight to usher in the dawn of a new age of peace. All that needed to be done has been completed and now, through our intervention, the dream of Operation Thor is about to become a reality.

"The path that we have chosen to follow has not been an easy one. The fact that we've lost more than forty NFA members since yesterday proves that. But, friends, let me tell you this. No job is ever worth doing if it's not worth doing your best.

"And so, here we are, the cream of the NFA crop." Hardy popped another mint into his mouth and tucked it inside his cheek as if it were a wad of chocolate tobacco. "Outside these doors, waiting to ride with us to the airport, are two dozen of our brothers and sisters, all of whom are as dedicated to a Nuclear Free Australia as we are.

"But before that can happen, before we can present to the world the beauty that is Operation Thor, we must decide which of us will have the honor of sacrificing his or her life in the name of global peace."

Hardy signaled, and Cheswick carried over a small wooden box lined with black velvet. Hardy accepted the box and then continued his speech.

"As I call your name, you are to come forward, reach into the box and retrieve one of the eleven gelatin capsules contained inside. When we have all done so, I will give the word and we will each drop our capsules into the glasses of water set before us. The water in ten of the glasses will become blue. One will be colored red. The person with the red glass will be our official winner. Any questions?"

When there were none, Hardy called upon Sheryl Galloway to begin the draw. She was quickly followed by her fellow New Zealander, Douglas Rice. Next came Trevor Jenkins, the senior NFA leader from Perth.

C. L. Roberts took his turn after that. Though technically not a member of Nuclear Free Australia's governing board, Roberts had requested and been granted the right to participate in the draw—a privilege reserved for only the highest ranking NFA members. Roberts solemnly made his selection, then returned to his seat as Cheswick approached Hardy.

"Good luck, Lawrence," Hardy said.

Cheswick dipped his hand into the black velvet box, but instead of picking up one of the remaining gelatin capsules, he removed all three, leaving in their place a pair of capsules that he had held in his palm. As Cheswick stepped away, Hardy presented the box to Thompson.

"We saved the best for the last, Ronald," Hardy told the bean-pole figure to his right. "Two capsules left. Yours and mine. Please make your choice."

As if he was reaching into a jar of deadly scorpions, Thompson scooped out one of the last two capsules and held it in his hand. Hardy inverted the black velvet box, and the final capsule rolled onto the table in front of him. He pushed the box to the side and lifted his capsule between forefinger and thumb.

With his free hand, Hardy felt around in his pocket for another cherry liqueur mint as well as for something else he had planted there prior to entering the room. He made a show of unwrapping the mint and slipping it into his mouth, then smiled broadly.

"You may now place the capsules in the glasses before you," Hardy announced.

While everyone at the table complied with the order, Hardy brought his hands together over his glass and released a capsule into the water. Then he crumpled his mint wrapper into a tiny foil ball and threw it, along with the other capsule that Thompson could have chosen, into a metal trash bin on the floor near his feet.

Staring expectantly, first one and then another of the group held their breath as the water in their respective glasses changed from crystal clear to a deep royal blue. Then the water in Thompson's glass began to change, prompting the skinny man to choke back a sob of despair. His face drained of color.

"Congratulations!" Hardy proclaimed, watching with everyone else as Thompson's water turned pink, then darker, until it finally obtained the color of rich red wine. "And to think, Ronald, if you had not chosen that capsule, the honor of unleashing Operation Thor upon the world would have been mine!"

Fully prepared to offer Hardy the opportunity he had narrowly missed, Thompson was caught off guard as his colleagues, their voices laced with relief, congratulated him on his good fortune.

"I know I'm not alone, Ronald," Hardy said once the well-wishing fervor had quieted, "when I say that I envy you. We all do. Yours is a deed that will be remembered forever. Your name will be synonymous with the cause of global peace for generations to come."

"Cheswick," Hardy said. "If you please."

Cheswick nodded and handed Thompson a silver tray on which had been placed an envelope and a small rectangular object that was not much larger than a cigarette pack.

"Inside the envelope is your ticket for this evening's gala at the opera house," Hardy instructed. "When our meeting concludes, you will go to the opera house and take your seat for tonight's performance.''

Hardy indicated the second object on the silver tray. ''At precisely 9:15, you will remove this radio-remote detonator from your pocket and activate it, doing so simply by pressing the button located on its side. This will detonate the bomb that we have sealed within the walls of the building. It will unleash the explosive power of approximately one thousand metric tons of TNT. Because of you, Ronald Thompson, Operation Thor shall live!''

Thompson gulped and was about to remove the envelope and detonator from the silver tray when the muffled sounds of automatic weapon fire could be heard. Instantly, an alarm was triggered, filling the conference room with the screaming noise of a siren.

Cheswick rushed to the window behind Hardy and drew aside the curtains. ''My God!'' he exclaimed, letting the curtains fall as he ran back to Hardy. ''We're under attack, Sebastian! Someone's attacking your estate!''

Hardy popped the last of his after-dinner mints into his mouth and then flipped a switch in the control console that was nestled within the arm of his chair. Hidden drawers immediately slid open in front of each of his guests. Inside each of the drawers was a gun.

Thompson gingerly lifted the revolver as though it might bite and stammered, ''What...what are we expected to do with these?''

Hardy swallowed the last of his chocolate mints and answered with a single word.

"Kill," he said.

25

The two cars sped toward Sebastian Hardy's palatial estate. Phoenix Force and Lila Blake rode in the first vehicle, a Ford Fairlane, while the second car carried six crack ASIO agents. Both groups expected to encounter trouble and had armed themselves accordingly.

Hardy's home was located in Point Piper, one of Sydney's most exclusive neighborhoods. The area featured some of the highest priced real estate in the city, including many properties that ran right up to the waters of Sydney Harbour. Hardy's home was no exception. Built on the largest singly owned plot of land in the neighborhood, Hardy's hideaway was large enough for ten families.

En route from the airport, Phoenix Force and their ASIO companion had received confirmation over their car's two-way radio that Sebastian Hardy had chartered a jet for a flight destined for Auckland, New Zealand. The flight was scheduled to depart Kingsford Smith Airport at 8:30 that night.

"The rotter's up to no good," McCarter said by way of an understatement. With Lila Blake providing directions, the team's Cockney member was driving at a breakneck, stomach-jumping pace. "He shouldn't suspect that we're onto him, so why pull a runner?"

"It's not a spur-of-the-moment decision," James noted. "Lila's people said the jet Hardy has chartered was reserved in his name more than a month ago."

"Which eliminates us as a cause for Hardy's trip," Katz concluded, feeling his equilibrium start to slide as McCarter whipped their vehicle in and out of Sydney's evening traffic. "No, if the jet was chartered more than thirty days ago, Hardy's trip to New Zealand must tie in with something else. But what?"

"Rats deserting a ship?" Manning guessed.

"That would especially hold true if every passenger scheduled to make the trip with Hardy was a member of the NFA," Hahn added.

"Yes," Lila Blake said, "but if the rats *are* deserting the ship we had better find out why. What could be so dangerous that Hardy and his friends want to be out of Sydney when it happens?"

"We'll know the answer to that question soon enough," Katz said, recalling the directions Lila had rattled off to McCarter upon their departure from the airport. "We take a right just ahead. Correct?"

The ASIO woman replied, "Yes, and Sebastian Hardy's home is not too far after."

"I doubt that Hardy will appreciate us postponing his traveling plans," Katz said just before they arrived.

"Too bad," McCarter commented. "After what happened to us in Darwin, I'm in the mood to cancel a few reservations."

Less than five minutes later, Phoenix Force and company were rolling up the tree-lined drive leading to Hardy's home. They had scarcely entered the boundaries of the property when three gun-toting NFA hit men suddenly materialized. The three men waved their weapons, warning the approaching cars to stop.

"Speed bumps at twelve o'clock," James noted, preparing to aim his Colt Commander out his rolled-down window.

"Save your bullets," McCarter advised, flooring the accelerator and sending their car rocketing forward. "This one's on me."

When the NFA sentries realized that the intruders had no intention of stopping, one Nuclear Free Australia tough guy made a do-or-die bid for survival by raising his auto rifle to fire. He was squeezing the trigger of his gun when he was struck and killed by the mean machine under McCarter's command.

The dead man's pals followed his lead. One sentry bounced off the hood of the Ford and flew headfirst into the trunk of a tree. Vertebrae snapped as if they were crisp breadsticks. The final NFA gunman was sucked beneath the Fairlane's wheels and crushed to death.

"See?" McCarter said. "Nothing to it. Three up. Three down. Who knows? Maybe that's the lot of them? Maybe we caught Hardy's NFA with their pants down?''

The Englishman skidded around a curve in the drive and brought his party face-to-face with twenty-one NFA killers looking for blood.

''Bugger all!'' McCarter exclaimed. ''Wrong again.''

Enemy bullets thudded into the side of the Ford as McCarter cut the wheel sharply to the right and sent the Fairlane leaping between the row of trees that lined the drive. The ASIO vehicle running backup made a similar move in the opposite direction; the combined action of the cars forcing the NFA welcoming committee to divide and separate.

Once through the trees, McCarter tapped the brakes and turned left, allowing the Ford to straddle a cobblestone walkway that ran parallel to the drive. Overhead lamps illuminated the narrow path. McCarter fed more gas to the engine, and the Ford responded with more speed.

As the Phoenix team and Lila Blake rode along the path, two more NFA devotees stumbled into view. One of the gunmen managed to fire his revolver once, the hastily aimed shot smashing into the side mirror near McCarter's elbow. The gunman corrected his aim and set his sights on the center of McCarter's chest.

''Some other time, sunshine,'' the British commando advised.

David McCarter stomped on the gas pedal. The Ford slammed into the flesh and blood obstacles. The

Fairlane's passengers caught a fleeting glimpse of broken bodies falling beneath the wheels as the car continued to roll on.

A double-barreled shotgun delivered twin blasts of searing destruction. The Ford's front tires exploded in unison, and McCarter found himself driving on rims. The Briton gritted his teeth and fought for control. The shotgunner broke his weapon open to dump the spent shell casings. McCarter saw the man try to shove fresh shells into the shotgun. The Briton turned the wheel and steered the Ford straight for the gunman. He heard the terrorist scream and felt the car bounce on impact. The Fairlane came to a halt directly over the body of the gunman.

An anguished scream came from beneath the car. The Ford's four doors opened. Phoenix Force and their ASIO associate piled out. Thirty yards ahead loomed Hardy's stately home, the three-story structure bathed in the glow of multiple floodlights.

Stepping over a severed hand that still clutched the shotgun, Manning turned suddenly as six NFA hoods came crunching through the brush. Slung over the brawny Canadian's shoulder was his H&K G-3 SG-1 sniper rifle, but it was the .357 Desert Eagle in his right fist that saved his life. Tracking his opponents' arrival by the amount of noise they were making, Manning opened fire with his Magnum the second his enemies materialized.

Two of the six NFA fanatics died swiftly, carrying enough Eagle lead in their guts to knock the pair off their feet and into their makeshift graves before they knew what had hit them. Their bodies were tumbling to the ground when the NFA hotshot holding down position number three singled out Manning for a one-way ride of death. The assassin changed his mind after one of the Eagle's slugs splattered his face and reno-vated the back of his skull. The gunman made a pa-thetic reach for the stars before falling to the earth.

"Gary!" McCarter shouted.

Heeding his friend's warning, Manning dropped below the side of the Ford, giving McCarter a clean line of fire on the last three killers. The Londoner's MAC-10 came to life, ripping the hapless recipients of his attention to bloody shreds in a flurry of 9 mm slugs. All three targets perished while trying to make sense of the hell that surrounded them.

Gunshots erupted as the ASIO agents backing up Phoenix Force clashed with the NFA on their side of the drive. Wary of further resistance, the Stony Man crew and Lila Blake took advantage of their enemies' distraction and hurried up the cobblestone path.

The Israeli colonel looked at the floodlights cover-ing Hardy's home and shook his head. Under such conditions, attempting to approach the building without being seen was impossible. Anyone venturing beneath the glare of the lights was inviting disaster.

Katz motioned Manning forward. "Kill the flood-lights."

"Consider it done," Manning said.

Holstering his .357, the Canadian unslung his Heckler and Koch G-3 SG-1. Equipped with a twelve-inch silencer and a Starlite night scope, the rifle was the perfect complement to Manning's skills as a sniper. Manning brought the stock of the rifle to his shoulder, aimed and fired. The H&K coughed in response, and one of the floodlights outside Hardy's house was destroyed in a combination of popping electricity and tinkling glass.

Five more times Manning fired. When he was finished, Sebastian Hardy's home was wrapped in a shroud of black.

"Shall we?" Manning asked.

"Let's," Katz said.

SEBASTIAN HARDY HAD WATCHED as the floodlights surrounding his home were eliminated one by one. He felt an uncontrollable urge to rush to the kitchen and prepare himself a sandwich. For once in his life he regretted his obsession with food. A war was being fought on the grounds of his estate, and he could only think about eating.

"What are we going to do?" Thompson whined, his voice climbing an octave with the sound of each additional gunshot. "We're trapped in here. Trapped! See where your crazy schemes have gotten us."

"Shut up!" Hardy ordered. "We will be fine if we just keep our heads."

"I know who's out there," Thompson loudly proclaimed. "It's the group from Darwin and Dunk

Island. They've killed everybody else, and now they've come here for us.''

''I told you to shut up!'' Hardy shouted his order again, this time with sufficient conviction to pierce Thompson's overwhelming fear.

Inwardly disgusted by Thompson's panic-stricken reaction to the situation, Cheswick asked, ''How many of them do you think we're facing, Sebastian?''

''Enough to know this is the end of the NFA movement if we don't play our cards right,'' Hardy said. ''Our people outside are obviously proving ineffective, otherwise the floodlights would still be functioning.''

''What do you suggest we do?'' Douglas Rice asked.

''Why not surrender?'' Thompson interrupted. ''It's our only hope. Then no more lives will be lost.''

''You're dead anyway,'' Hardy declared. ''So quit complaining. Once you unleash Operation Thor, you'll cease to exist.''

Thompson threw the radio-remote detonator onto the conference table. ''That's insane. They're not going to allow us to get to the opera house. They're going to kill us all right here.''

''So why wait?'' Hardy demanded, his stomach growling as he pointed his gun at Thompson and fired twice. ''You're a coward and a bore. Good riddance!''

Ronald Thompson stared bleakly at the double splotches of blood staining the breast pocket of his starched white shirt. He blinked at the sea of faces growing faint before his eyes, then sagged into his seat as a river of red flowed onto his shirt.

Momentarily stunned by Hardy's unexpected actions, Sheryl Galloway regained her composure as she asked, "What now? What about Operation Thor?"

"Leave that to me." Hardy snatched the detonator with his left hand. "While the rest of you hold off our enemies, Cheswick and I will make our way to the opera house. We will have to sacrifice our lives for the successful completion of Operation Thor."

"Preposterous!" Jenkins exclaimed. "Anyhow, you'll both be shot before you reach the end of your drive."

"Only if Lawrence and I take the conventional route," Hardy countered.

"Meaning?" Jenkins asked.

"We'll take my speedboat across the harbour," Hardy said. "If we can depend upon you to cover us until we can get the boat going, there's no reason that Operation Thor has to be canceled. What do you say?"

Thompson breathed his last and slumped facedown onto the conference room table.

"Well?" Hardy repeated, waving his gun.

"All right," Jenkins agreed for the group. "You and Cheswick had better leave now. We'll delay our opponents for as long as we can."

"Excellent," Hardy said with as much emotion as his growling stomach would allow. "God bless you all. We'll meet again."

With the radio-remote detonator in one hand, and a Walther P-5 pistol in the other, Hardy engineered his exit from the room with Cheswick tailing close behind.

"Do you really think we can make it, Sebastian?" Cheswick asked once he and Hardy had made their departure.

Hardy nodded grimly as he took a detour through the kitchen. "Of course."

UNDER THE COVER OF DARKNESS, the Phoenix five and Lila Blake quickly covered the distance separating them from Hardy's home. Ten yards away they saw the silhouette of a figure holding a gun outlined against the curtains of a window on the building's first floor.

"I've got him," James said, lashing out with a pair of Colt Commander .45 heartstoppers.

The window cracked, and the armed silhouette fell forward against the curtain. The curtain pulled free, and both it and the dead man fell over the windowsill and dropped to the ground.

A gunman Gary Manning recognized as C. L. Roberts showed himself long enough to snap off a couple of shots. One bullet drilled into the dirt at Karl Hahn's feet, while the other came within a quarter inch of nipping McCarter in the thigh. The West German and

Englishman met the attack with some firepower of their own, sending a shower of lead through the hollow space of the missing window, transforming the interior of Hardy's conference room into a veritable death chamber.

About to yell for someone to switch off the lights, C. L. Roberts had just opened his mouth to speak when four bullets from Hahn's MP-5 canceled the order. Stitched through the side of his chest and across his jaw, Roberts did an impromptu backflip onto the conference room table and died.

Two additional H&K slammers caught Douglas Rice just as he was about to run out the door. He reached for the knob, then lost the will or the ability to live after the back of his skull disintegrated. A fleeing Sheryl Galloway tripped over her countryman's corpse and buried her head in her hands.

Trevor Jenkins screamed and knew he would never see Perth again when three Ingram slugs from McCarter's MAC-10 slammed into his rib cage. Fire blossomed in the older man's lungs, and he coughed and spit blood. Summoning all of his remaining energy, Jenkins clenched and squeezed the trigger of his gun.

Jenkins collapsed to his knees as his pistol discharged, its bullet traveling less than five feet before striking the cold flesh of C. L. Roberts. The wounded man from Perth coughed again and then sank to the carpeted floor.

Silence filled the room, and the NFA female from New Zealand gingerly lifted her arms from her head and looked around. Sheryl Galloway knew that everyone else was dead.

Outside, the battle between the ASIO backup unit and their NFA adversaries was gradually turning in favor of the outnumbered ASIO. Although they had suffered two casualties, the ASIO agents had inflicted losses three times greater on the NFA.

The steady reduction of their ranks had a demoralizing effect on several of the NFA gunmen; it encouraged them to seek their fortunes elsewhere. Leaving behind those still wishing to fight, a number of the men beat a hasty retreat farther onto Hardy's property.

Out of range of the ASIO strike team, the five deserters broke into a run that brought them to the end of the tree-lined drive directly opposite Hardy's home. They were so intent on making good their escape that they practically found themselves standing face-to-face with Phoenix Force before realizing their mistake.

Katz fired his Uzi into the NFA gunman leading the retreat group. The man was ripped open from crotch to sternum. One of the enemy fired a shot at Lila Blake. She felt a slight tug at the fabric of her blouse. The ASIO female agent responded by pumping two .38 Special rounds through the chest of her opponent. The bullets burst his heart as if it were a blood-filled balloon.

Calvin James dived to the ground as subgun fire sought to boot the American warrior down the road of death. James hit the lawn, rolled to the right and rose in a kneeling position with his Colt Commander held in a two-hand Weaver combat grip. He fired two rounds, blasting both .45 slugs through the upper torso of the machine gunner. The gunman went down forever, but another NFA assassin charged forward and lashed a kick to James's forearm that sent the pistol flying.

"Not again," James growled, annoyed that he had been disarmed once more.

The Aussie fanatic who had delivered the kick, swung the stock of a Marlin lever-action rifle at James's head. The guy had either run out of ammo, or his weapon had jammed. Either way, he had been forced to use his rifle as a club. James dropped sideways to avoid the walnut stock. His right leg lashed out, and his boot slammed into the terrorist's face.

The kick propelled the terrorist backward and sent him directly into the line of fire as more NFA creeps tried to blast Gary Manning. The fanatic's body twisted and jerked as high-velocity rounds smashed into his flesh from both sides. The butchered terrorist fell to earth as another NFA deserter swung his assault rifle toward Gary Manning.

The Canadian triggered his Eagle pistol. A .357 slug burst into the gunman's belly, drilled through his innards and tore out a kidney. The terrorist screamed and doubled over as Manning fired another .357 message of destruction. The 158-grain wad-cutter split the top of the Aussie killer's skull. His corpse tumbled to the lawn.

The last NFA killer to stumble upon Phoenix Force was wishing that he had stayed to fight ASIO instead. Karl Hahn and David McCarter caught the trapped gunman in a ruthless cross fire of 9 mm parabellums. Bullets ripped into his body, left, right and center. The killer was reduced to a bloodied rag doll before his body collapsed in a twitching heap on the lawn.

The front door to Hardy's home flew open, and Sheryl Galloway charged out, her pistol seeking any target it could find. Lila Blake and Gary Manning whirled to confront the newest NFA threat. Manning's shot blew away a meaty chunk of the Galloway woman's right thigh. Lila's .38 slug nailed the New Zealander through the shoulder.

Galloway cried out as she lost her balance and dropped her weapon. She spilled to her hands and knees, then collapsed facedown on the walkway leading from the door. She gasped and twisted on her side, dividing her attention between the two dreadful wounds.

"You bastards think you've won, but you're wrong!" she snarled. "You got everybody but Hardy and Cheswick." She laughed in spite of her pain. "You'll never stop them now. You're too late. Hardy has the detonator. Hardy will destroy you all!"

James suddenly pointed. "What the hell's that?"

As they looked in the direction James indicated, a four-wheeled vehicle not much larger than a jeep came speeding from behind Hardy's home and onto a narrow strip of pavement running from the house toward the shore of the harbour. McCarter emptied the Ingram's magazine at the moving target and, though the Cockney's aim was true, all of the MAC-10's bullets ricocheted off into space.

"Damn!" James swore. "The sucker's armor-plated."

"Come on," Manning said, beginning to run. "Hardy must have a boat docked out back."

"The lady you and Lila plugged says this Hardy clown's got a detonator," James said, keeping pace with Manning. "A detonator to *what*, though?"

"I don't want to find out the hard way," Manning returned, increasing his speed as the rapidly retreating vehicle carrying Hardy and Cheswick vanished around a curve in the pavement strip.

Even before he reached the curve, the Canadian heard the distinct sounds of dual engines roaring to life. When Manning rounded the bend, he saw Hardy and Cheswick pulling away from a dock in a high-powered speedboat. Cheswick was at the wheel of the craft, while a triumphantly gleeful Hardy was shaking his fist at his pursuers.

Manning ran to the end of the dock and stopped, hoping there would be another boat he could use to give chase. There was none. By now Hardy and Cheswick were one hundred yards out into the harbour and turning on a course toward the Sydney Opera House.

"Hold this," Manning said, tossing his Eagle in the air. James caught the .357 as Manning whipped his H&K G-3 SG-1 from his shoulder.

Hardy and Cheswick gained another twenty-five yards as Manning brought the sniper rifle's Starlite scope to his eye. He swept the scope across the harbour, searching the boats on the water until he had Hardy's boat in his sights. Manning blinked and lined up his shot, his task made more difficult by the way the speedboat rose and fell as it skimmed over the water.

Through the scope Manning could see Hardy's enormous form as the founder of the Nuclear Free Australia movement held out his right arm to the opera house in the distance. With his free hand, Hardy was stuffing something into his mouth.

When the boat was two hundred yards from shore, Manning fired at it, maintaining eye contact with the Starlite scope as he fired again. Hardy's body jerked almost immediately as the first .223 Remington bullet connected with the fat man's hip. The second G-3 mini-rocket hit home, and Hardy's arms began flapping as something that he was holding in his right hand fell from his grasp.

Hardy leaned forward in a bid to catch the falling object just as the speedboat tilted unexpectedly. Hardy fell overboard into the cool dark waters. The speedboat slowed and circled, but by then Sebastian Hardy had already sunk to the bottom of Sydney Harbour.

Manning relaxed and lowered his rifle as Katz and the others ran to the end of the dock.

"Did you get Hardy?" Katz asked.

Manning nodded. "He just took a dive about two hundred yards out. The big guy went under and stayed there."

"What about the detonator?" Hahn asked.

"A small radio transmitter?" the Canadian inquired, and Hahn nodded. "It went overboard with Hardy."

"Then the NFA has been put out of the terrorist business permanently," Katz declared. "And that wraps up our mission, gentlemen."

EPILOGUE

Lawrence Cheswick surrendered without a fight and was taken into custody by ASIO. Confronted with the overwhelming failure of Operation Thor, the prisoner revealed everything he knew about the NFA's mad scheme to detonate the stolen backpack bomb in order to destroy Sydney.

Sheryl Galloway, the only other NFA survivor of the battle at Sebastian Hardy's estate, refused to comment on anything Cheswick said, verbally branding the man a liar and a traitor. She was still proclaiming the glories of the Nuclear Free Australia movement as she was sedated and prepped for surgery.

LILA BLAKE DROVE Phoenix Force to Kingsford Smith Airport for their return flight to the United States. Katz, Hahn, James and McCarter said their goodbyes and then boarded the plane.

"So," Manning said. "I guess this is it, Lila. For now, anyway."

"Does that mean I'm going to see you again, Gary?"

"Between your line of work and what I do, I think we're talking a definite maybe."

"Forget about that. I'm talking about us. Maybe we made a mistake years ago by slipping away from each other."

"I know. I've been thinking the same thing. Seeing you again brought it all back, Lila. But things are different now. I'm in no position to make any promises."

"I'm not asking for promises, Gary. If it's going to happen, it will happen. Just give it some thought."

"I will," Manning said as the final boarding call for his flight was announced. "Well, I have to go. I . . . come here."

Manning pulled the unresisting woman into his arms and held her tight as their lips met in a kiss. "Take care of yourself, Lila," the Canadian finally said.

"You, too," the woman told him. "See you around. Don't make it so long next time."

Then she kissed Manning again and was gone.

RAFAEL ENCIZO WAS FINISHING a set of leg lifts when Colonel Towers entered the room.

"I thought I'd find you here," Towers said.

"What's up, Doc?" Encizo asked as he stepped down from the leg lift machine.

The surgeon held up a folder. "I thought you might want to take a look at these."

"Oh?" Encizo asked. "What's that?"

Colonel Towers smiled. "Your walking papers."

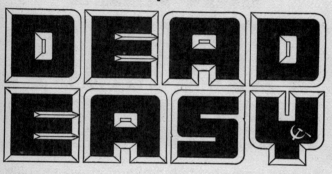

WATCH FOR

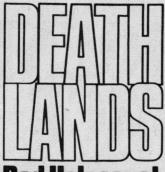

DEATH LANDS
Red Holocaust

WHEN ALL IS LOST,
THERE'S ALWAYS THE FUTURE

But the future in a world shrouded in the radioactive
red dust clouds of a generation-old global nuclear war
depends on finding hidden caches of food, weapons
and technology—the legacy of a preholocaust
society—stashed in lonely outposts known as redoubts.

When Ryan Cawdor discovers a redoubt in the bitter
freakish wasteland that now passes for Alaska, he also
uncovers a new threat to a slowly reemerging America.

Roaming bands of survivors have crossed the Bering
Strait from Russia to pillage Alaska and use it as the
staging ground for an impending invasion of America.

In the Deathlands, the war for domination is over, but
the struggle for survival continues.

**DEATHLANDS: Adventure and Suspense in
the Midst of the New Reality**   DL2

Mack Bolan's

PHOENIX FORCE

by Gar Wilson

The battle-hardened, five-man commando unit known as
Phoenix Force continues its onslaught against the hard
realities of global terrorism in an endless crusade for
freedom, justice and the rights of the individual. Schooled
in guerrilla warfare, equipped with the latest in lethal
weapons, Phoenix Force's adventures have made them a
legend in their own time. Phoenix Force is the free world's
foreign legion!

**"Gar Wilson is excellent! Raw action attacks
the reader on every page."**
—Don Pendleton

4 FREE BOOKS
1 FREE GIFT
NO RISK
NO OBLIGATION
NO KIDDING

SPECIAL LIMITED-TIME OFFER

Mail to Gold Eagle Reader Service

In the U.S.
901 Fuhrmann Blvd.
P.O. Box 1394
Buffalo, N.Y. 14240-1394

In Canada
P.O. Box 2800, Station A
5170 Yonge St.,
Willowdale, Ont. M2N 6J3

YEAH! Rush me 4 free Gold Eagle novels and my free mystery bonus. Then send me 6 brand-new novels every other month as they come off the presses. Bill me at the low price of just $14.95— a 13% saving off the retail price. There are no shipping, handling or other hidden costs. There is no minimum number of books I must buy. I can always return a shipment and cancel at any time. Even if I never buy another book from Gold Eagle, the 4 free novels and the mystery bonus are mine to keep forever.

Name _____ (PLEASE PRINT)

Address _____ Apt. No. _____

City _____ State/Prov. _____ Zip/Postal Code _____

Signature (If under 18, parent or guardian must sign)

This offer is limited to one order per household and not valid to present subscribers. Price is subject to change.

166-BPM-BP6F

NO-SUB-1-RRR

TAKE 'EM NOW

FOLDING SUNGLASSES FROM GOLD EAGLE

Mean up your act with these tough, street-smart shades. Practical, too, because they fold 3 times into a handy, zip-up polyurethane pouch that fits neatly into your pocket. Rugged metal frame. Scratch-resistant acrylic lenses. Best of all, they can be yours for only $6.99. **MAIL ORDER TODAY.**

Send your name, address, and zip code, along with a check or money order for just $6.99 + .75¢ for postage and handling (for a total of $7.74) payable to Gold Eagle Reader Service, a division of Worldwide Library. New York and Arizona residents please add applicable sales tax.

Remove from pouch...

unfold once...

unfold twice...

and they're ready to wear.

**Gold Eagle Reader Service
901 Fuhrmann Blvd.
P.O. Box 1325
Buffalo, N.Y. 14240-1325**

Offer not available in Canada.

1. How do you rate _____ ?
   (Please print book TITLE)
   - 1.5 ☐ excellent   .3 ☐ good   .1 ☐ poor
   - .4 ☐ very good   .2 ☐ fair

2. How likely are you to purchase another book in this series?
   - 2.1 ☐ definitely would purchase   .3 ☐ probably would not purchase
   - .2 ☐ probably would purchase   .4 ☐ definitely would not purchase

3. How do you compare this book with similar books you usually read?
   - 3.1 ☐ far better than others   .4 ☐ not as good
   - .2 ☐ better than others   .5 ☐ definitely not as good
   - .3 ☐ about the same

4. How did you *first* become aware of this book?
   - 8. ☐ read other books in series   11. ☐ friend's recommendation
   - 9. ☐ in-store display   12. ☐ ad inside other books
   - 10. ☐ TV, radio or magazine ad   13. ☐ other _____
     (please specify)

5. What *most* prompted you to buy this book?
   - 14. ☐ read other books in series   17. ☐ title   20. ☐ story outline on back
   - 15. ☐ friend's recommendation   18. ☐ author   21. ☐ read a few pages
   - 16. ☐ picture on cover   19. ☐ advertising   22. ☐ other _____
     (please specify)

6. Please check the statements you feel best describe this book.
   - 25. ☐ Easy to read   35. ☐ Too much violence
   - 26. ☐ Realistic conflict   36. ☐ Interesting characters
   - 27. ☐ Original plot   37. ☐ Not enough humor
   - 28. ☐ Story was too short   38. ☐ Didn't like the subject
   - 29. ☐ Good humor in story   39. ☐ Fast paced
   - 30. ☐ Liked the subject   40. ☐ Difficult to read
   - 31. ☐ Too predictable   41. ☐ Story was too long
   - 32. ☐ Not enough description of setting   42. ☐ Believable characters
   - 33. ☐ Couldn't put the book down   43. ☐ Not enough suspense
   - 34. ☐ Slow moving   44. ☐ Unrealistic conflict

7. Have you any additional comments about this book?
   _____
   _____

8. What types of books do you usually like to read?
   - 47. ☐ Mystery   50. ☐ Espionage/Spy   52. ☐ Action/Adventure
   - 48. ☐ Horror   51. ☐ Science Fiction   53. ☐ Westerns
   - 49. ☐ War

9. Have you purchased any books from any of these series in the past 12 months? Approximately how many?

	No. purchased		No. purchased
☐ Mack Bolan	(55) _____	☐ War Dogs	(63) _____
☐ Soldier of Fortune	(56) _____	☐ Able Team	(64) _____
☐ Saigon Commandos	(57) _____	☐ The Destroyer	(65) _____
☐ Death Merchant	(58) _____	☐ The Black Eagles	(66) _____
☐ SOBs	(59) _____	☐ The Assassin	(67) _____
☐ The Survivalist	(60) _____	☐ Vietnam: Ground Zero	(68) _____
☐ Nick Carter	(61) _____	☐ Phoenix Force	(69) _____
☐ TNT	(62) _____	☐ Michael Sheriff: The Shield	(70) _____

10. Please indicate your age group and sex.
   - 78.1 ☐ Male   79.1 ☐ under 15   .4 ☐ 23-26   .7 ☐ 35-49
   - .2 ☐ Female   .2 ☐ 15-18   .5 ☐ 27-30   .8 ☐ 50-64
   -      .3 ☐ 19-22   .6 ☐ 31-34   .9 ☐ 65 or older

Thank you for completing and returning this questionnaire.

PF98765432

NAME _____
(Please Print)

ADDRESS _____

CITY _____

ZIP CODE _____